guarded by shadows
The Protector Series
Book Two

viggo vaughn

Guarded by Shadows
The Protector Series - Book 2
Copyright © 2025 by Viggo Vaughn
All rights reserved.

Book Cover and formatting provided by Trisha Fuentes
https://bit.ly/m/trishafuentes

No part of this book may be reproduced in any form or by any electronic or mechanical means, including information storage and retrieval systems, without written permission from the author, except for the use of brief quotations in a book review.

ISBN: 979-8-3482-9930-9 (Paperback)

Published by
Ardent Artist Books
www.ardentartistbooks.com

about ardent artist books

➥ ABOUT US

Ardent Artist Books was established in 2008

We publish modern and historical romances once a month!

Get Your FREE List: Published & Upcoming Books
visit our website at:
https://bit.ly/3Wva4o0

* * *

➥ WE HAVE BOOK TRAILERS

Follow us on YouTube!
https://bit.ly/3W3xn7a

Like, Subscribe & Comment

* * *

➥ WE HAVE SERIALIZED FICTION!

Visit our website today to download one of our stories that unfold in bite-sized pieces!

Each installment is just 99¢!
Paperback $15.99

https://bit.ly/3LsDpJL

* * *

➥ LET'S CONNECT!

Fuel your love of fiction with exclusive content and captivating insights from Ardent Artist Books. Whether you crave the thrill of modern narratives or the timeless elegance of historical fiction, our newsletter delivers a curated selection straight to your inbox. Plus, as a welcome gift, receive a FREE downloadable eBook:

"The Family Fix"

https://bit.ly/49BR3UB

contents

Prologue	1
1. Mia's Ordinary Life	7
2. Enzo's Dilemma	17
3. Worlds Collide	27
4. Dangerous Games	37
5. A Trapped Bird	47
6. A Daring Escape	57
7. The Unraveling	67
8. Discovery	77
9. The Reckoning	87
10. Tension in the Air	95
11. Giovanni's Fury	105
12. Breaking Point	115
13. The Hunt Begins	123

you might also like

The Dark Side of Him	133
Read Next	135
The Bargain Bride	137
Second in Command	139
Evenly Matched	141
About Viggo Vaughn	143
Also by Viggo Vaughn	145

prologue

...

The bell above the diner door jangled as Enzo Falchetti swaggered inside, his designer shades perched atop his artfully tousled hair. He slid into a corner booth, sprawling across the red vinyl seat like he owned the damn place.

A pretty little waitress hurried over, ponytail bobbing. "What can I get for you today?"

Enzo flashed her a panty-dropping grin, running an appreciative gaze over her curves. "Loaded bacon cheeseburger, extra fries, chocolate milkshake. And your number."

She blushed prettily, ducking her head. "I'll get your order right out."

While he waited, Enzo drummed his fingers on the table, restless energy thrumming through him. Being the youngest son of a mafia king came with a certain expectation of chaos and trouble. One he was always happy to fulfill.

His food arrived in record time, the waitress casting him flirty glances beneath her lashes. Enzo winked at her before diving in, devouring the juicy burger and crispy fries like a starving man.

Halfway through his meal, raised voices caught his attention. He glanced over to see two beefy *guidos* in cheap suits hassling the pretty waitress. One grabbed her arm, trying to drag her towards the back.

Enzo was out of his seat in a flash. "I believe the lady isn't interested, fellas." His tone was casual, but laced with steel.

The men spun to face him, meaty fists clenched. "Mind your business, pretty boy."

A feral grin curved Enzo's mouth. He rolled his shoulders, cracking his neck side to side. "See, here's the thing. This pretty boy is Enzo *fucking* Falchetti. And I'm making it my business."

Recognition flickered in their beady eyes, followed swiftly by fear. They released the waitress, backing away with hands raised. "We don't want no trouble with the Falchetti's."

"Then get the fuck out of my sight before I decide to redecorate this dump with your brain matter."

They couldn't scramble out the door fast enough. Enzo turned to the waitress with a softer smile. "You okay?"

She nodded, eyes wide and cheeks flushed. "Thanks for the save. I'm Mia, by the way."

"I'm the guy who's gonna be starring in your dreams tonight." He brushed a finger down her cheek, gratified when her pupils dilated and her breath hitched.

Mia bit her lower lip, a mixture of nerves and excitement swirling in her warm brown eyes. "Does that line usually work for you?"

Enzo chuckled, the sound low and intimate in the space between them. "Wouldn't know. Never had to use it before."

She raised a skeptical brow. "Right. I'm sure you have women falling all over you without even trying."

"What can I say? It's a gift." He shrugged, the movement showcasing the lean muscles beneath his designer shirt. "But maybe I've just been waiting for the right woman to try a little harder for."

A pretty blush stained her cheeks, but she held his gaze. "And you think that's me?"

Enzo leaned in closer, his voice a husky murmur. "I think there's only one way to find out. Let me take you out, beautiful. Show you what it's like to be wined and dined by a Falchetti."

Mia's breath caught, her pulse fluttering wildly at the base of her throat. She knew the smart thing would be to walk away. Getting involved with the mafia was a one-way ticket to heartbreak...or worse. But damn if every cell in her body wasn't screaming at her to throw caution to the wind and take a walk on the wild side for once in her life.

"One condition," she said, surprising them both. "No wining and dining. I want the real Enzo, not some suave mafioso act."

His brows shot up, but a genuine smile tugged at the corners of his mouth. "The real Enzo, huh? You sure you can handle that?"

The challenge in his tone sent a shiver down her spine. Mia lifted her chin. "Guess you'll have to wait and see."

"Guess I will." Enzo's smile sharpened into something hungry and full of promise.

"Meet me out front after your shift. Wear something you don't mind getting dirty. We're gonna have some real fun, Mia mine."

He tossed a wink over his shoulder as he swaggered out of the diner, leaving Mia flushed and tingling in anticipation of the night to come. *What the hell had she just gotten herself into?*

Mia's shift seemed to drag on forever, the minutes ticking by with agonizing slowness. She couldn't stop thinking about Enzo and the heat in his eyes when he'd issued that challenge. *The real Enzo.* The thought sent a forbidden thrill through her veins. She knew he'd be just a fling, but oh how she was looking forward to every topple.

As she wiped down tables and refilled coffee cups, Mia's mind wandered to dangerous places. She imagined Enzo's rough hands on her body, his lips trailing fire along her skin. She pictured him taking her hard and fast, claiming her in a way no man ever had before.

By the time her shift finally ended, Mia was wound tighter than a piano wire. She clocked out in record time, hastily changing into a pair of dark jeans and a tank top that hugged her curves like a second skin.

Heart pounding, she stepped out into the balmy evening air to find Enzo waiting for her, leaning against a sleek black motorcycle. He looked like every bad boy fantasy come to life, all tousled hair and wicked smiles.

"Hop on, baby," he said, tossing her a helmet. "Hope you're ready for the ride of your life."

Mia caught the helmet, adrenaline surging through her bloodstream. *This was crazy. Reckless.* The kind of thing good girls like her didn't do.

To hell with being good.

She straddled the bike behind Enzo, molding her body to his

back. The rumble of the engine between her thighs was nothing compared to the need pulsing in her core.

Enzo revved the throttle and they took off into the night, the city lights blurring around them. Mia held on tight, surrendering to the rush of speed and danger and sheer, unadulterated want.

She had no idea where Enzo was taking her, but at that moment, she didn't care. For once in her life, Mia was ready to embrace the unknown - and the man who embodied it.

mia's ordinary life
...
A MONTH LATER

mia ricci

The fluorescent lights of Tony's Diner hum overhead as I wipe down the counter for the hundredth time today. My regulars filter in and out - the construction workers with their coffee-stained thermoses, the elderly couple who split a slice of apple pie every afternoon, the rushed businesspeople who barely look up from their phones.

"Here you go, Mr. Peterson. Extra crispy bacon, just how you like it." I slide the plate in front of the retired mailman who's been coming here since before I started.

"You're an angel, Mia." His weathered face crinkles into a smile.

I return his warmth, even as my feet ache in these worn-out sneakers. Six years ago, I dreamed of writing bestselling romance novels. Now, I'm twenty-six and lucky if I can squeeze in a few paragraphs between shifts. But dreams don't pay the bills, and since losing Mom and Dad, staying afloat has been my only priority.

The bell above the door chimes. A group of men in expensive suits walk in, their presence immediately changing the atmosphere. The other customers seem to shrink into their booths. I've seen their type before - the ones who carry power like a visible weight on their shoulders. They take the corner booth, the one partially hidden by a partition.

"Coffee?" I approach with my pot, keeping my voice steady.

One of them waves me away without looking up. I catch fragments of their hushed conversation as I retreat - something about territories and warnings.

The morning drags on as I move between tables, collecting sticky plates and half-empty coffee cups. My mind wanders while my body works on autopilot - grab dishes, wipe table, reset places. The suits in the corner booth remain deep in conversation, their coffee growing cold.

"Order up!" My boss' voice booms from the kitchen. I balance three plates along my arm - a skill perfected through countless shifts.

"Club sandwich, no tomatoes." I set the first plate in front of a woman in scrubs. "Double cheeseburger, extra pickles. And chicken Caesar, dressing on the side."

The lunch rush hits like a tidal wave. The bell above the door chimes every few minutes, bringing in waves of hungry office workers, construction crews, and shopping mall employees. The diner fills with the clatter of cutlery and overlapping conversations.

Between orders, I let my mind drift to pristine beaches and crystal-clear waters. I close my eyes for a split second and imagine warm sand between my toes, the sound of gentle waves replacing the chaos of the diner. No coffee stains on my apron, no screaming kids throwing french fries, no mysterious men in expensive suits...

"Miss? Can I get another coffee?"

Reality snaps back. My tropical escape dissolves into fluorescent lights and linoleum floors.

"Coming right up." I grab the coffee pot, weaving through the maze of tables and chairs.

The suits are still here, their voices growing louder as more empty glasses collect on their table. My feet throb in my sneakers as I dash from the kitchen to the dining room, delivering plates of steaming burgers and fresh salads. The notepad in my pocket is filled with scribbled orders, each page a reminder of dreams deferred.

I catch my reflection in the chrome napkin dispenser - wisps of hair escaping my ponytail, a smudge of ketchup on my uniform. In my daydreams, I'm lounging in a hammock, laptop open, writing stories about passion and adventure. Instead, I'm here, refilling sugar dispensers and explaining why we can't substitute sweet potato fries for regular ones.

"Where's my tuna melt?" A man at table six waves his empty plate.

"Just checking on that for you, sir." I hurry to the kitchen window. "Boss, how's that tuna melt coming?"

The lunch rush swallows my island fantasy whole. My shoulders tense as I carry plates, my smile fixed in place as I handle complaints about cold coffee and overcooked eggs. The suits in the corner grow more animated, their voices carrying across the diner in sharp bursts before dropping to whispers.

I imagine palm trees swaying in a warm breeze, and the sound of exotic birds calling from the dense jungle. Somewhere far from this cramped diner, far from the weight of responsibility and the ghost of forgotten dreams. A place where I could write without interruption, where characters could come alive on the page instead of dying in the notes app on my phone.

"Miss? We need more napkins at table four."

"Right away." I grab a stack of napkins, my bare island slipping away like sand through my fingers.

The lunch crowd pulses with hungry impatience. I move faster, my feet knowing the path between tables without conscious thought. The bell keeps ringing, the kitchen keeps churning out orders, and my tropical escape remains just out of reach - a mirage shimmering beyond the grease-streaked windows of Tony's Diner.

The dinner rush dies down around nine. I'm in the back storage room, counting napkin boxes, when the first gunshot cracks through the air. My heart stops. More shots follow, along with screams and the sound of shattering glass.

Moving on autopilot, I press myself against the wall and inch toward the kitchen door. Through the narrow window, I see them - three men with guns drawn, standing over a body sprawled across the checkered floor. Blood spreads across white tile like spilled wine.

"Check the back," one orders.

I stumble backward, knocking into a shelf. A can crashes to the floor.

Their heads snap toward the sound.

My breath catches as one of them spots me through the window. Our eyes lock for a split second before I bolt toward the emergency exit.

The night air hits my face as I burst into the alley. Footsteps thunder behind me. I run faster than I've ever run, my waitress uniform constraining my movements. I take random turns through familiar streets that suddenly feel alien and threatening.

When I finally stop, gasping for air in another alley, a shadow detaches itself from the darkness. My heart nearly explodes when one of the men grabs me.

My scream dies in my throat as strong hands grab my wrists, yanking them behind my back. The grip is like iron, crushing my bones together. I thrash and kick, but it's useless against his strength.

"Got you now, sweetheart." His breath is hot against my ear.

Rough fabric swoops over my head - his coat, engulfing me in darkness and the scent of expensive cologne mixed with gunpowder. I can't see, can barely breathe through the heavy material. My heart pounds so hard I think it might burst.

"No, please—" The words come out muffled. I try to shake the coat off, but he holds it firmly in place.

My feet leave the ground as he lifts me. I kick wildly, connecting with something solid. A grunt of pain, then a sharp curse.

"Feisty little thing, aren't you?" Another voice, closer now. "The trunk's open."

The trunk. *No, no, no.*

I twist harder, throwing my whole body into fighting their grip. My elbow connects with flesh. Someone swears. A hand tangles in my hair through the coat, yanking my head back.

"Stop struggling or this gets worse for you."

They lift me higher. For a moment, I'm suspended in darkness, my stomach dropping like I'm on a roller coaster. Then I'm falling, landing hard on cold metal that knocks the breath from my lungs. My hip slams against something rigid - probably the spare tire.

The coat shifts, letting in a sliver of streetlight. Before I can move or scream, the trunk slams shut with a definitive clang. The sound echoes through my bones like a death knell.

Darkness. Complete, suffocating darkness.

The engine roars to life. We're moving, tires squealing against pavement. My body slides with each turn, bouncing against the trunk walls. The space is so tight I can barely move, can't get my hands free. Every bump in the road sends pain shooting through my trapped arms.

I try to count the turns - left, right, right again - but lose track as panic claws at my throat. The coat is still half-wrapped around my head, making it hard to breathe. The trunk smells like motor oil and leather, with undertones of something metallic that might be blood.

My mind races with horrible possibilities. That man in the diner, lying in a pool of blood. *Is that my fate too?* The image of his blank eyes haunts me as we speed through the night.

The car takes another sharp turn. My head hits something hard, and stars explode behind my eyes. I taste copper in my mouth - must have bit my lip. Or maybe my cheek. Everything hurts too much to tell.

Voices drift back from the front seat, muffled by distance and engine noise:

"Boss wants her at the house."

"She saw too much."

"Falchetti will decide what to do with her."

Falchetti. The name strikes a chord of terror. Everyone knows that name, even if they pretend not to. The family that rules the city's underworld with an iron fist. The ones you never want to cross.

And now they have me.

We hit a pothole and I bounce hard against the trunk lid. Pain shoots through my shoulder. I try to curl into a ball, to protect myself from the next impact, but there's no room. My muscles scream from being trapped in this awkward position.

The car speeds up. Wind whistles through some tiny gap, creating an eerie howl. Or maybe that's just in my head. My thoughts scatter like leaves in a storm - Mom and Dad's faces, my unfinished novel saved on my laptop, Mr. Peterson who will wonder why I'm not there to serve his eggs tomorrow.

Another turn sends me sliding. The coat shifts again, covering my face completely. I can't breathe. Can't think. The darkness is absolute now, pressing in from all sides like a living thing.

The car's speed changes - we must be on a highway now. The ride smooths out but the engine's growl grows louder. My whole world narrows to this metal coffin, to the thunder of blood in my ears and the rasp of my breathing through expensive fabric.

I should have taken that job in Seattle last year. Should have listened when Jenny said the diner wasn't safe anymore. Should have done anything but walk into that storage room at exactly the wrong moment.

The car swerves suddenly. My head cracks against something again and lights dance behind my eyes. This time, the darkness that follows isn't from the coat or the trunk. It rises from inside me, threatening to pull me under.

No. I have to stay awake. Have to keep fighting. Have to...

Another bump. Another wave of pain.

enzo's dilemma
. . .

enzo falchetti

Standing in the dimly lit study of the Falchetti estate, my muscles tense as I watch our soldiers file in. The failed hit wasn't supposed to go this way. Blood rushes in my ears as they deliver their report to Dante.

"There's a witness," one of them says, his voice grating on my nerves. "A waitress at Mario's Diner."

My stomach drops. *Mario's Diner.* I know that place. I spent countless nights there, watching her move between tables with that gentle smile. *What was her name?* The memory of soft skin and whispered promises floods back. One perfect night, then we both moved on. Or so I thought.

"Bring her in," Dante orders, his voice cutting through my thoughts.

The soldiers drag in a figure, coat over her head, hands bound behind her back. Despite the rough treatment, she doesn't struggle or cry. The calm surprises me - most people would be hysterical.

"Remove it," Dante commands.

The coat comes off, and my world stops spinning. Dark waves tumble around her shoulders. Those big brown eyes that once looked at me with such heat now flash with defiance. Mia. The name hits me like a punch to the gut.

Dante's gaze travels down her length, assessing. My jaw clenches. I want to step between them, block his view. The urge is irrational, dangerous.

"Well," Dante says, "what do we have here?"

Mia lifts her chin, refusing to be cowed. The same spirit I glimpsed that night at her apartment when she matched my passion with her own. Now it could get her killed.

I watch Mia, my mind racing. *How the hell did she end up here?* Just weeks ago, she was safe behind that diner counter, untouched by our world. One chance encounter with our family's business, and now she's bound in our study like a sacrificial lamb.

My brother's cold stare rakes over her again. Every muscle in my body screams to intervene, but I force myself still. One wrong move could make this worse.

"You saw something you shouldn't have," Dante says, circling her like a shark. "Tell me exactly what you witnessed."

The soldiers shift uncomfortably. They fucked up - badly. Standard protocol is to clear civilians before any hit. Instead, they let loose in an occupied diner. Amateur hour bullshit that's left us with a witness and a mess to clean up.

"I was in the storage room," Mia says, her voice steady despite everything. "I heard shouting, then gunshots."

My hands curl into fists. The storage room. Of course - where they keep the extra coffee supplies. I remember that tiny space, remember pressing her against those shelves that night, her laugh turning to gasps as I—

Focus. This isn't about that night. This is about right now, about keeping her alive.

"And then?" Dante prompts.

"I looked out. Saw your men shooting at someone. There was so much blood..." She swallows hard but maintains eye contact with my brother. Either incredibly brave or incredibly stupid. Maybe both.

I study the soldiers, memorizing their faces. Heads are definitely going to roll for this clusterfuck. We're not amateurs - we're the fucking Falchetti family. Hits are supposed to be clean, precise. Not this spray-and-pray bullshit in a public diner.

"The target?" Dante asks the soldiers.

"Got away," one mumbles. "We winged him, but..."

I bite back a groan. Jesus Christ. Not only did they fail to clear civilians, they missed their mark? Father is going to lose his shit when he hears about this.

"So let me understand this," I speak up, unable to stay silent any longer. "You didn't secure the location. You failed to eliminate the target. And now we have a witness?" My voice drips with disgust. "What's next - you gonna post about it on social media?"

The soldiers pale. Good. They should be scared.

"Enzo," Dante warns, but I'm not done.

"No, brother. This is fucking amateur hour. We're better than this." I gesture at Mia. "She shouldn't be here. None of this should have happened."

Mia's eyes find mine, and for a split second, I see recognition flash across her face. Does she remember that night too? The way we moved together, the promises we whispered in the dark? I force the memories away. They're dangerous - for both of us.

"What do you suggest we do about it?" Dante asks, his tone dangerous.

I know what he's thinking. There's only one way the Family usually handles witnesses. But the thought of Mia ending up in the river makes my blood run cold.

"Let me handle it," I say, choosing my words carefully. "I'll make sure she understands the consequences of talking."

"You?" Dante's eyebrow rises. "Since when do you volunteer for cleanup?"

Since I spent a night learning every inch of her skin. Since I discovered what her laugh sounds like at 3 AM. Since I walked away thinking I'd never see her again.

"Since our soldiers proved they can't handle basic operations without fucking everything up," I say instead. "Someone needs to clean up their mess. Might as well be me."

Dante studies me for a long moment, his dark eyes unreadable. I hold his gaze, praying he can't see through me. Can't see how my heart is hammering against my ribs, how every fiber of my being is screaming to get Mia out of here.

"Very well," he finally says. "But Enzo?" His voice drops low. "Don't make me regret this."

* * *

mia ricci

My hands ache from the zip ties digging into my wrists as I step into what has to be the most intimidating entrance hall I've ever seen. Crystal chandeliers drip from coffered ceilings, their light dancing across marble floors that probably cost more than I'll make in ten lifetimes. The grandeur only amplifies my fear.

"Move." Enzo's voice is low behind me, his hand firm on my lower back.

I stumble forward, my sneakers squeaking against the pristine floor. God, even my footsteps sound out of place here. Ornate mirrors line the walls, reflecting back a terrified version of myself - disheveled brown hair, wide eyes, and work uniform still stained with coffee from my shift.

"Please," I whisper, turning to face Enzo. "You don't have to do this. Whatever you think I saw—"

"Quiet." His hazel eyes flash with something that might be regret, but it's gone before I can be sure. He guides me down a hallway lined with what looks like original paintings.

We enter a study that screams old money - leather chairs, dark wood paneling, shelves of leather-bound books. Enzo closes the door behind us with a soft click that sounds like a prison gate slamming shut.

"The zip ties," I say, holding up my bound wrists. "They're cutting off my circulation."

"They stay on."

"Seriously? After everything that happened between us that

night?" I throw the words at him like weapons, watching his jaw clench. "You're really going to treat me like this?"

"That night was a mistake." His voice is cold, controlled. "This is business."

"Business?" I laugh, but it comes out more like a sob. "You kidnapped me from my job and brought me to your family's mansion. How is this business?"

"I'm trying to protect you."

"Protect me? By holding me hostage?"

The fight drains from me as I really look at him. Enzo leans against his father's mahogany desk, arms crossed over his chest. The tailored black suit can't hide his athletic build, and those hazel eyes that once sparkled with mischief now burn with intensity. My heart skips, remembering.

That night at the diner started so innocently. Him, ordering coffee after closing. Me, wiping down tables. The electricity when our eyes met. The way he followed me into the storage room, pressing me against the shelves. His motorcycle rumbling beneath us as we sped through empty streets, the wind whipping my hair while I clung to his leather jacket.

"You can't even look at me now?" I challenge, watching his jaw tighten. "After everything?"

"That was different." His voice is rough. "We were different people then."

"Were we? Or are you just playing the role your family expects?"

He pushes off the desk, crossing to the window. Moonlight catches his profile - the strong jaw, the slight curl of dark hair at his neckline. "You don't understand what's at stake here."

"Then help me understand! One minute you're this charming guy who makes me laugh, who looks at me like..." I swallow hard. "And now you're acting like some cold-blooded—"

"Because that's what I am, Mia." He whirls to face me. "That night was a fantasy. This is reality. My family, my obligations—"

"Your obligations?" I step closer, ignoring how my heart races. "What about your obligation to basic human decency? To treating people like they matter?"

"You think I don't—" He cuts himself off, running a hand through his hair. "Christ, Mia. You have no idea how much I'm risking just keeping you alive right now."

The words hit me like a slap. "So I should be grateful? That the great Enzo Falchetti spared my life?"

"Yes!" His composure cracks. "Because anyone else in my family would have put a bullet in your head the minute you saw what happened at that diner!"

We're toe to toe now, both breathing hard. The same magnetic pull from that first night crackles between us. His eyes drop to my lips for a fraction of a second before he jerks away.

"I'm trying to protect you," he says, quieter now. "Even if that means you hate me."

"I don't hate you." The words slip out before I can stop them. "I hate this situation. I hate feeling powerless. I hate that the guy who made me feel so..." I bite my lip. "He seems gone."

"He has to be gone." Enzo's voice is barely above a whisper. "For both our sakes."

The grandfather clock in the corner ticks away the heavy silence. I study his rigid posture, the tension in his shoulders. He's fighting something - maybe the same memories that keep flooding back to me. The tenderness in his touch. The way he'd looked at me like I was precious. Worth protecting.

"My brother's coming." His head snaps toward the door. "Remember what I said - keep quiet and let me handle this."

My bound hands tremble. "Enzo—"

"Trust me." For just a moment, I see a flash of the man I met that night. "Please."

The sound beyond the door vanishes.

Enzo runs a hand through his dark hair, messing up its perfect style. "You don't understand what you've gotten yourself involved in."

"Then explain it to me!" I yank against the zip ties in frustration, wincing as they bite deeper into my skin.

He paces the length of the study, conflict written across his handsome features. Finally, he stops and faces me. "The man who was killed tonight? He wasn't just some random target. He was connected to the Moretti family."

The name hits me like a physical blow. Everyone in the city knows about the Morettis - the other major crime family, the Falchettis' biggest rivals.

"Oh God." My legs go weak and I sink into one of the leather chairs. "So I didn't just witness a murder, I witnessed…"

"A hit. Part of an ongoing war between our families." Enzo's voice is grim. "And now you're caught in the middle of it."

I stare up at him, this man who just hours ago I'd thought of as the mysterious stranger from that passionate night we shared. Now he stands before me as something entirely different - a mafia heir holding my life in his hands.

"What are you going to do with me?" I ask, hating how my voice trembles.

His eyes meet mine, and for a moment I see a flash of the man I'd connected with that night - gentle, almost vulnerable. But then his expression hardens again, the mask of the Falchetti enforcer sliding back into place.

"Whatever it takes to keep you alive."

worlds collide
. . .

mia ricci

The sharp plastic edges of the zip ties dig into my wrists as Enzo spins me around. His fingers wrap around my bicep, firm but not painful. My heart skips when I catch the glint of steel - a knife appearing from his back pocket. The blade slides between my skin and the plastic, and with a quick movement, he cuts through the restraints.

"Don't try anything stupid," he mutters, his breath warm against my ear.

I rub my wrists, trying to restore circulation. The red marks are already forming angry welts across my skin. "Like what? Make a run for it past your small army down there?"

His grip returns to my arm, steering me through the sprawling hallway. Men in dark suits line the walls like sentries, their faces hard and expressionless. But their eyes follow my every move. Some wear barely concealed weapons - the bulge of a holster beneath a jacket, the outline of a knife at an ankle. My stomach churns. *How many people in this mansion are trained killers?*

"Eyes forward," Enzo commands when he catches me staring.

The grand staircase stretches before us, its mahogany railings gleaming under crystal chandeliers. But it's the walls that capture my attention. Countless faces stare back at me from ornate frames - generations of the Falchetti crime family preserved in photographs and oil paintings.

A black and white wedding photo shows a stunning bride in vintage lace beside a stern-faced man. Their features echo in the faces of children in other photos - formal portraits of boys in suits, and family gatherings around holiday tables. Some photos are recent enough that I recognize a younger Enzo, his rebellious smirk already in place.

"Your family?" I ask, my voice barely above a whisper.

"Keep moving." He nudges me forward, but I can't tear my eyes away from the visual timeline climbing the walls.

The older portraits grow more elaborate - oil paintings of distinguished men and women in period clothing. Their eyes seem to follow us, judging, questioning my presence in their domain. A particularly imposing portrait draws my attention - a man who could be Enzo's great-grandfather, his hand resting on an ornate chair while a beautiful woman stands beside him. The artist captured a hardness in his eyes that sends a chill down my spine.

The deeper we move into the mansion, the more I understand. This isn't just a wealthy family's home—it's a fortress, a seat of power built on generations of influence and violence. The photos aren't just decoration; they're a warning, a reminder of the legacy I've stumbled into.

"Those marks on your wrists will fade," Enzo says suddenly, breaking the silence. "Other choices might leave more permanent scars."

I swallow hard, hearing the threat beneath his words. My skin burns where he touches me, and not just from fear. I remember that night - the electricity between us, the way his hands felt different then. But that was before I knew who he really was, before I witnessed what his family is capable of.

We pass more armed men on the upper landing. Their reverent nods to Enzo speak volumes about his position here. The young rebel I thought I knew that night is also this - heir to a criminal empire, trained in violence, capable of ending lives with the same hands that once traced patterns on my skin.

The hallway seems endless, lined with more photos, more history, more proof of just how deep and far-reaching the Falchetti influence stretches. A recent family photo catches my eye - Enzo standing with who I assume is his father and brother. The family resemblance is striking, but while his father and brother's expressions are hard and controlled, there's something different in Enzo's eyes. Something that matches the hesitation I felt in him at the diner.

"Quite the family tree," I manage to say, trying to keep my voice steady despite my racing heart.

"Some branches are better left unpruned," he responds cryptically, his grip tightening slightly as we pass another group of armed men.

I focus on my breathing, on keeping my steps even. Each face on the wall, each armed guard we pass, each twist and turn through this labyrinth of power and danger reinforces one terrifying truth: I'm trapped in a world I never knew existed, surrounded by people who view my life as nothing more than a loose end to be tied up.

I step into the guest suite, and my breath catches. The room is bigger than my entire apartment, dripping with luxury I've only seen in magazines. Crystal chandeliers cast warm light across silk wallpaper and plush Persian rugs. A king-sized bed dominates one wall, topped with more pillows than I could count.

"Your clothes are in the closet," Enzo says from behind me. "Everything you need should be here."

I walk to the massive walk-in closet, running my fingers over designer labels I could never afford on a waitress's salary. "This is... excessive."

"It's necessary. You'll be here for a while."

A while. The words hit me like a punch to the gut. This beautiful room is still just another kind of cell. I move to the window, taking in the sprawling grounds below. Heavy iron bars mar the view.

"The bathroom has everything you need too." Enzo's voice is softer now, almost apologetic. "Toiletries, makeup..."

I spin around, anger flaring. "So I can look pretty while I'm being held captive?"

"You're not a captive. You're under protection."

"Tampons?"

He gives me a smirk, "Everything's there. You're under *protection*." He repeated, getting angry.

"Right." I gesture to the bars. "Because all protected people need to be caged."

He runs a hand through his dark hair, frustration evident. "The security is as much for your safety as it is to keep you here. There are cameras in the main room and by the doors. The bathroom and closet are private."

Of course, they're watching. I walk to the bathroom, needing space. It's as luxurious as the rest - marble everything, a shower big enough for four people, and a soaking tub that looks like it belongs in a spa.

"I'll have dinner sent up," Enzo says from the doorway.

"Playing the gracious host now?" The words come out bitter, but I can't help it. Everything about this situation is wrong.

"Mia..." He takes a step forward, then stops himself. "I know this isn't ideal. But it's the best I can do right now."

I turn to face him, taking in his troubled expression. For a moment, I see flashes of that night we shared - his gentle touch, the way he'd looked at me like I was something precious. But that was before I knew who he really was. Before I became a liability to his family.

"The best you can do?" I laugh, but it sounds hollow. "You've locked me in a gilded cage because I saw something I shouldn't have. Don't pretend this is for my benefit."

His jaw tightens. "You don't understand the danger you're in. What the Morettis would do-"

"What about what your family would do?" I cut him off. "I saw the look in your father's eyes. I'm just a loose end to him."

Enzo's silence speaks volumes. He moves to the door, pausing with his hand on the handle. "Try to get some rest. I'll check on you later."

The door closes with a soft click, followed by the unmistakable sound of a lock engaging. I sink onto the edge of the massive tub, my legs suddenly weak.

The marble is cold against my palm as I steady myself. Everything in this room probably costs more than I make in a year, but all I can think about is how far I am from my simple apartment, my normal life. From freedom.

A glance in the mirror shows my reflection - still in my waitress uniform, looking small and out of place among all this luxury. Cameras are watching my every move. Armed guards probably patrol outside. And somewhere in this mansion, a family of killers decides my fate.

* * *

THE VIBRANT SUNSET casts long shadows through the window as I gaze down at the perfectly manicured gardens below. My new "home" is as beautiful as it is terrifying - a gilded cage where every luxury reminds me I'm a prisoner.

The door bursts open, making me jump. Enzo strides in, his hazel eyes stormy. "My father wants you at dinner. Now."

My stomach drops. "What? No, I can't—"

"This isn't a request." He runs a hand through his tousled dark hair. "Listen, just... follow my lead. Say as little as possible."

Ten minutes later, I'm seated at an enormous mahogany table that could host twenty people. Tonight it's just four - Giovanni at the head, Dante to his right, Enzo beside me. The silence is deafening as servers bring out the first course.

"Ms. Ricci." Giovanni's voice is smooth as aged whiskey, but there's steel underneath. "I trust you're finding your accommodations satisfactory?"

"Yes, thank you." I force myself to meet his calculating gaze.

"Good. Now perhaps you can explain exactly what you saw that night at the diner."

Enzo shifts beside me. "Father, is this really—"

"Quiet." Giovanni doesn't even look at his son. His steel-gray eyes remain fixed on me.

I take a slow sip of wine, buying time to steady my nerves. "I was in the storage room when I heard the shots. When I looked out, I saw three men in suits. One was on the ground." I keep my voice even, though my heart pounds. "That's all."

"And you didn't recognize anyone?"

"No."

Giovanni's lip curls slightly. "You're lying."

"Father—" Enzo starts again.

"I said quiet!" Giovanni's fist hits the table, making the crystal glasses jump. "Ms. Ricci, let me be clear. Your continued comfort—your continued breathing—depends entirely on your honesty."

I feel Enzo tense beside me, but something inside me snaps. "You want honesty? Fine. I recognized your son's face from our previous... encounter. And I saw enough to know your family handles problems with bullets. But I'm not stupid enough to go to the police, and I'm not naive enough to think I'd survive trying to blackmail you. So here I am, eating osso buco with the man who's deciding whether to kill me. How's that for honest?"

Dead silence falls. Dante's dark eyes narrow. Giovanni's

expression is unreadable. Only Enzo moves, his hand finding mine under the table and squeezing once.

Finally, Giovanni's mouth twitches. "Well. Perhaps there's more to you than meets the eye, Ms. Ricci."

The rest of dinner passes in a blur of expensive wine and careful conversation. Hours later, Enzo walks me back to my room. As soon as the door closes, my legs give out and I sink onto the plush carpet.

"Hey." Enzo crouches beside me. "You did good in there. Better than good."

"I thought he was going to shoot me right there at the table."

"My father appreciates backbone, even if he'd never admit it." Enzo sits beside me, our shoulders touching. "Where did that come from anyway? I've never seen anyone stand up to him like that."

"Guess losing everything once makes you less afraid of losing it again." The words slip out before I can stop them.

His eyes soften. "Your parents?"

I nod, surprised to find tears threatening. "Car accident. Four years ago. They were everything to me."

"I lost my mother when I was twelve. Cancer." His voice roughens. "The family had all this money, all this power, but we couldn't save her."

I turn to look at him, really look at him. In the dim light, his usual swagger is gone, replaced by raw vulnerability that makes my heart ache. His face is inches from mine, and I can't help but remember that night months ago - the heat of his skin, the taste of his lips.

"Mia..." he breathes, and I know he's remembering too.

dangerous games

...

mia ricci

From my cozy corner in the mansion's library, I try to lose myself in the leather-bound volumes surrounding me. The rich scent of old books fills my nose, almost masking the lingering hints of gunpowder and danger that seem to permeate every corner of this gilded prison.

Enzo leans against a mahogany bookshelf, his presence both unsettling and magnetic. "Found anything interesting?"

"Just wondering if any of these books have secret passages behind them." I trail my fingers along the spines. "That's how it works in all the stories, right?"

A ghost of a smile plays on his lips. "You're the writer. You tell me."

"Used to be. Haven't written much since..." The words catch in my throat.

"Since your parents?" His voice softens, and for a moment, I see past the mafia heir to the man I spent that one passionate night with.

"Dreams feel silly when you're just trying to survive." I move closer, watching his body tense. "What about you? Any childhood dreams before daddy dearest groomed you for the family business?"

His jaw tightens. "We don't all get choices, Mia."

"Don't we?" I step into his space, close enough to catch the spicy scent of his cologne. "You made a choice with me. Twice now."

"That was different." His eyes darken as they drop to my lips.

"Was it?" I press my hand against his chest, feeling his heart race beneath my palm. "Or are you just afraid to admit you want something for yourself?"

"Mia." My name comes out as a warning, but his hands find my waist.

"What's wrong, Enzo?" I lean in, letting my breath brush his neck. "Scared of the waitress?"

His fingers dig into my hips. "You're playing with fire."

"Maybe I like getting burned." I drag my nails down his chest, remembering how he'd responded to my touch that night.

He catches my wrist, his control visibly fraying. "Stop."

"Make me." I press closer, letting my body meld against his. "Or are you too afraid to—"

A deafening crack splits the air. Glass shatters somewhere outside.

Enzo moves with lightning speed, pushing me down behind a heavy desk. "Stay down!"

I hit the floor as another shot rings out. Enzo rushes to the window, his body tense and alert.

"What's happening?" My heart pounds against my ribs.

"Drive-by." He peers through the curtains. "Our guys are responding."

Shouts and more gunfire erupt from the front of the mansion. I can hear the thunder of boots on gravel, the sharp commands being barked across the grounds.

"I see them," Enzo mutters, his hand pressed against the window frame. "They're heading toward the south gate. Marco! Get those cars moving!"

I resist the urge to peek, remembering how well that worked out for me at the diner. "Are they..."

"Moretti's men." His voice is steel. "Has to be."

* * *

enzo falchetti

The study feels suffocating, tension crackling through the air like static before a storm. Father sits behind his mahogany desk, fingers steepled under his chin as Dante paces the Persian rug. My shoulder still throbs from earlier - a reminder of how close we came to disaster.

"They knew exactly when to strike." I grip the back of a leather chair, knuckles white. "The timing was too perfect."

"Of course they did." Dante's voice carries an edge sharper than any blade. He pulls something from his jacket pocket - a crushed bullet, its metal warped and twisted. "Found this in what's left of the Mercedes."

Father takes it, turning it over in his palm. His expression darkens as he reads the engraving. "**'The girl is dead.'** Seems the Morettis are sending us a message."

My jaw clenches. The image of Mia's terrified face flashes through my mind - how she'd trembled against me during the attack, her fingers digging into my arms. "They won't touch her."

"Getting protective, little brother?" Dante's tone holds a warning.

"She's under our protection now. My protection." The words come out harsher than intended. "If they want to get to her, they'll have to go through me first."

Father's phone buzzes. His face remains impassive as he reads the message, but I catch the slight tightening around his eyes. Without a word, he turns the screen toward us.

Sofia Moretti's name glows at the top: "Consider this a warning, Giovanni. The waitress dies, or your entire empire burns. Your choice."

"Dramatic as ever," Dante mutters, but there's no humor in his voice. "Dumb bitch."

"She's made her move." Father sets the phone down with deliberate care. "The question is why? What makes this girl so important?"

I think back to the night at the diner, to what Mia might have seen. There has to be more - something we're missing. "Whatever it is, Sofia wants her dead badly enough to risk open war."

"Which makes Ms. Ricci either very valuable..." Father's gaze locks with mine. "Or very dangerous."

"Or both," Dante adds.

My fingers itch to check on Mia, to make sure she's still safe in her room. The weight of what we're facing settles heavy on my shoulders. Keeping her alive just got exponentially more complicated.

"I want everything we have on Sofia's recent movements," Father orders. "Every contact, every business deal, every whispered rumor. If she's willing to break the peace over this girl, I want to know why."

"I'll handle it," Dante says, already pulling out his phone.

"And the girl?" Father's attention returns to me.

"She stays with me." The words come out before I can stop them, fierce and certain. "Twenty-four-seven protection. No one gets near her without going through me first."

Father studies me for a long moment, his expression unreadable. "Very well. But remember, Enzo—she's a liability. Don't let your..." He pauses meaningfully. "...protective instincts cloud your judgment."

The warning is clear. Don't get attached. Don't let feelings compromise the family. But as I think of Mia upstairs—her quiet strength, the way she faces each new horror with determination despite her fear—something shifts in my chest.

"I understand my responsibilities," I tell him, careful to keep my voice neutral. But internally, I'm already mapping out security protocols, identifying weak points, planning escape routes. I'll keep her safe, whatever it takes.

"Sofia's not subtle," Dante says, looking up from his phone. "If she's coming for the girl, she'll make it bloody."

"Then we'll be ready." I straighten, rolling my shoulders back. "Double the guards. Install new security systems. Change up the patrol routes. No one gets within a mile of this house without us knowing."

Father nods slowly. "Handle it. But remember—this is bigger than one girl now. Sofia's made her play. How we respond will determine the future of this family."

The weight of his words settles over the room. He's right - the stakes have changed. What started as a simple cleanup has evolved into something far more dangerous. And at the center of it all is Mia, somehow both our greatest vulnerability and potentially our strongest asset.

A text lights up my phone—the guard stationed outside Mia's door reporting in. She's safe, but restless. Pacing. My hands clench at the thought of her up there alone, probably terrified.

I almost miss my turn, but thankfully, my senses aren't dulled by liquor or exhaustion. After a quick nod to Falco, I make my way up the grand staircase, my mind whirling with the danger that looms over us all. This was never about territory or business deals - it's personal now, and that makes my blood sing in ways I can't quite understand.

When I reach Mia's door, I knock softly before hearing a muffled voice from within. "Come in." It's quieter than I expect, barely audible over the frantic thumping of my heart. As soon as it opens, my attention locks onto her. She's curled into a tight ball on the hardwood floor, her eyes wide and frightened.

"Enzo?" Her voice is just as shaky as her fingers as she reaches out to me. I nod, stepping inside and gently guiding her guard out of the room. As soon as the door closes behind us, locking us in, my protective instincts take over. "What's wrong?"

She shakes her head, gulping back tears. My heart clenches at the sight of her vulnerability - a softness so unlike anything I've seen before. Without a word, I kneel beside her, pulling her into a warm embrace that surprises us both. Her thin frame fits against me like a puzzle piece, and for a fleeting second, I forget about the Falchetti family and the threats against us. Her sobs shake us both as I stroke her hair, whispering soothing words in her ear until she catches her breath again.

When she pulls back, our faces are only inches apart. There's something different about her tonight - a fierceness that matches my own, making the air hum with anticipation. I can see it in her eyes as clearly as if it were written on her skin - she'll never be scared again if I can help it. My mind goes blank as we stare at each other, powerless against the pull between us.

And then, before I can think twice, she wraps her arms around my shoulders and pulls me down. Our lips meet in a searing kiss that sends shockwaves through my body. If I had any doubts before about the wisdom of this arrangement, they're gone now. This woman, this girl, is mine. My arms snake around her waist, pulling her closer until I can feel the beat of her heart against mine. She moans softly into my mouth, a low, throaty sound that ignites a fire deep within me.

Breathless and desperate, we stumble toward the bed, our clothes discarded one piece at a time. I watch in awe as she unfurls like a flower, every inch of her pale skin revealed under the soft light of the moon. Her nipples are already hard nubs against her shirt, begging for attention. I take one into my mouth, sucking gently as my hand explores lower, brushing against her soft hair.

Without further hesitation, I push her shirt up and over her head, tossing it aside. Her bra follows soon after. When my fingers brush over her smooth skin, she grips my hair tighter, arching into my touch. I can't help but tease her, tracing lazy circles around her nipples until they're hard little pebbles begging for more. My lips find her neck, while my other hand slides lower, finding the hem of her shorts.

I tug at the waistband, drawing it over her hips. She's wearing matching panties, barely there and already damp. I kiss her along her jawline, tasting her skin - so sweet and addicting. My tongue finds its way to her earlobe, tracing gentle circles that send shivers down her spine. In one swift move, I flip us over and climb on top of her. She gasps when my hardness presses against her soft, wet folds.

My kisses trail down her neck, over her collarbone, and to her breasts, where I tease her hard nipples with my teeth and tongue before taking them both into my mouth. I suck deeply, savoring the salty taste of her skin. She gasps and arches her back, her fingers digging into my back as if she needs more of me. I want to give it to her, wrap myself around her and never let go.

I trail kisses further down her stomach, taking my time to explore every inch of her. By the time I reach her panties, I'm already rock-hard, aching for her in a way that surprises even me. With a slow, teasing tug, I pull them off and she shudders beneath me. I bury my face between her legs, inhaling her scent that's both tangy and sweet, a mixture of fear and desire. Her taste is unlike anything I've ever known, electrifying and unforgettable.

I worship her, licking and sucking until she's squirming underneath me. When I can tell she's close, I move up her body, kissing my way up her thighs until I'm at eye level with her wet center. "Look at you, so beautiful," I murmur, running my thumb along her swollen folds. Her gaze meets mine, and in that instant, I know she's mine.

I place gentle kisses along her belly button, over her ribs, and up her chest before finally claiming her lips once more. This time, it's a possessive kiss, one that says she's mine and always will be.

Her palms roam freely over my back, setting off fireworks in my spine as we move together, skin against skin.

I position myself at her entrance and thrust deep, feeling her tighten around me instantly. She's soft and hot, like nothing I've ever known.

As we reach our peak, we fall apart, gasping for air. I'm dizzy with the taste of her, drunk on the feel of her body against mine. For a moment, we lie there, caught in the afterglow. She's the only thing real amidst the chaos of the mafia.

Reluctantly, I roll off her, taking a moment to catch my breath. "Thank you," she whispers, tracing circles on my chest.

"You're welcome," I reply, my voice rough. "Sleep now."

But sleep doesn't come easily to me tonight. Instead, I lie awake, thinking about Sofia Moretti and the danger she poses to our family. It seems like every time we think we've gained an inch, she strikes back harder than before. We need a new plan - something to tip the scales in our favor. But more importantly, we need to keep Mia safe.

a trapped bird

...

mia ricci

The steady tick of the ancient typewriter keys mocks me from across the room. I've been staring at the same spot on the wall for what feels like hours, watching dust particles dance in the beam of sunlight that cuts through the heavy curtains. Time has become elastic here - stretching and contracting without rhythm or reason.

My fingers trace the silk edge of the decorative pillow beside me. Everything in this room screams luxury, from the handwoven Persian rug to the antique furnishings. But it's all just prettier bars on my gilded cage.

"You can write your stories," Enzo had said when he brought in the typewriter, his voice soft but distant. That was... three days ago? Four? The days blur together now. He barely meets my eyes anymore when he checks on me, his visits becoming shorter and less frequent.

I miss him. The thought hits me like a physical ache in my chest. I miss the way he used to linger, how his presence filled the room with an energy that made me feel less alone. Now there's just... emptiness.

The bookshelf across the room holds dozens of leather-bound classics. I've read through most of them already, but the words have started to lose their meaning. Pride and Prejudice, Jane Eyre, Wuthering Heights - all these romantic heroines trapped in their own ways, just like me. At least they got their happy endings.

My throat tightens as I curl deeper into the window seat. Outside, the manicured gardens stretch toward the high stone walls. Guards patrol the perimeter like clockwork. I've memorized their rotation schedule, not that it matters. I'm not going anywhere.

The typewriter sits accusingly on the ornate desk, its blank page a reminder of my frozen creativity. I used to lose myself in writing, building worlds and characters that felt more real than reality. Now my imagination feels as locked up as I am.

A sound catches in my throat - not quite a sob, but close. I won't cry. I've done enough of that in the shower where no one can hear me. Instead, I press my forehead against the cool glass of the window, counting my breaths like the therapist taught me years ago after my parents died.

"One, two, three..." The numbers don't help. Neither does trying to remember how many days I've been here. Twenty? Thirty? The seasons haven't changed, but it feels like years have passed since that night at the diner.

My reflection in the window looks like a stranger - designer clothes I didn't choose, perfectly styled hair I maintain out of habit rather than desire. Even my eyes seem different, darker somehow. Or maybe that's just the shadows under them from another restless night.

The click of the door lock makes me tense, but I don't turn around. Probably just another guard with my meals, or maybe Maria coming to clean. They never speak to me anymore - Enzo's orders, I assume. The silence is becoming its own kind of torture.

Footsteps cross the room, too heavy to be Maria's. My heart quickens despite myself. Enzo? But they pass behind me without pausing, and I hear the bathroom door open and close. Just another security check then. Making sure I haven't somehow fashioned a weapon from hand lotion and cotton swabs.

The emptiness swells again when the footsteps retreat. The door locks with a final, decisive click. I pull my knees tighter to my chest, making myself smaller in the vast room. Everything here is too big, too grand, too much - except for the space I'm allowed to exist in, which shrinks a little more each day.

My gaze drifts to the typewriter again. The blank page seems to grow whiter, brighter, until it's all I can see. I should write something. Anything. Even if it's just Dear Diary, I'm losing my mind. But my body feels too heavy to move, weighted down by a fog that's been settling over me for days.

A bird lands on the windowsill outside - some kind of sparrow, I think. It tilts its head, studying me through the glass. For a moment, I imagine I can feel its freedom, taste the open air. Then it spreads its wings and disappears, leaving me alone with my reflection and the endless tick of a clock I can't see.

The monotony of luxury is still a prison. I pace the plush carpet of my gilded cage, tracing the same path I've walked for days. The guards stationed outside my door have become as familiar as furniture - their shifts, their habits, even their coffee breaks.

One of them, Rocco, catches my eye whenever I peek out. He's different from the others - younger, with kind eyes that betray a hint of sympathy whenever he sees me. Today, as he brings my breakfast tray, there's something else in his expression.

"Ms. Ricci." He sets down the tray, then hesitates. "I know this isn't easy for you."

I wrap my arms around myself, trying to hold in the loneliness that threatens to spill out. "I just... I miss my life. My friends probably think I'm dead."

Rocco glances over his shoulder, then pulls something from his jacket pocket. A small burner phone. "For emergencies only," he whispers. "Don't let anyone know you have it. If Mr. Falchetti finds out..."

My hands shake as I take it, sliding it into my robe pocket. "Thank you."

After Rocco leaves, I wait until the afternoon shift changes before pulling out the phone. My fingers hover over the keypad. I should save this for emergencies, but I need to know if anyone's looking for me. With trembling fingers, I dial my voicemail.

"You have three new messages," the robotic voice announces.

The first two are spam calls from before everything happened. But the third - my heart stops when I hear Gina's voice, recorded just hours ago.

"Mia, you have to come!" Her words tumble out in a panicked rush. "They're after me! I saw something I shouldn't have, and now they're watching me. I'm scared, Mia. I don't know who else to turn to. Help me Mia, help me. I'm hiding out at your place —where are you?"

A Trapped Bird

Ice runs through my veins. Gina sounds terrified, her usually cheerful voice cracking with fear. In the background, I hear what sounds like blinds being drawn, doors being locked.

I replay the message, pressing the phone harder against my ear. The same horror that gripped me that night at the diner now claws at my chest. Gina's seen something - something involving the Morettis. The same family that wants me dead.

My hands are shaking so badly I almost drop the phone. Gina's alone out there, trapped in the same nightmare I'm in, but without the dubious protection of the Falchetti family. I think of her apartment above that old bookstore, exposed and vulnerable.

I pace faster, my mind racing. I can't leave - the guards, the security systems, Enzo's watchful eyes - they're all designed to keep me here. But Gina's message echoes in my head, her terror becoming my own. She's my friend, maybe my only real friend in this city, and she's in danger because of the same world that's imprisoned me.

The burner phone feels heavy in my hand, a lifeline and a burden all at once. I should tell Enzo about this. He'd know what to do, wouldn't he? But then Rocco would be exposed, and I'd lose this one connection to the outside world. Plus, what if the Falchettis decide Gina is just another loose end to tie up?

I sit on the edge of my bed, clutching the phone like a lifeline. Through my window, I can see the manicured gardens of the estate - beautiful and suffocating. Somewhere beyond these walls, Gina is hiding, terrified and alone, just like I was before Enzo found me.

The irony isn't lost on me. I'm safer than I've ever been, surrounded by armed guards and protected by one of the most powerful families in the city. But my friend is out there, facing the same danger I escaped, begging for help I can't give.

I tuck the phone into the false bottom of my jewelry box - another luxury given to me by my captors. Every sparkly piece inside worth more than I used to make in a month at the diner. Now they serve a better purpose, hiding my secret connection to the outside world.

My fingers trace the intricate patterns on the box as Gina's message plays over and over in my mind. The taste of helplessness is bitter in my mouth. I'm trapped in this beautiful cage, unable to help the one person who's reaching out to me, while the shadows that hunted me now stalk my friend.

***

sofia moretti

From across the river, I watch the Falchetti mansion through my binoculars. Such an ostentatious display of wealth and power. My lip curls in disgust. The sun sets behind the tall windows, casting long shadows across the manicured lawn.

"Everything is in place, Ms. Moretti." Philo, my most trusted lieutenant, stands at attention beside me. "The waitress made the call exactly as instructed."

I lower the binoculars, satisfaction coursing through my veins. "And how is our guest doing?"

"Gina remains... cooperative. Amazing what the threat of harm to one's family can accomplish."

A cold smile plays at my lips as I recall the terrified waitress, trembling as she recorded the message for her friend Mia. The fear in her eyes when my men explained exactly what would happen to her elderly mother if she didn't comply. Sometimes the simplest plans are the most effective.

A Trapped Bird

"The phone?" I ask, though I already know the answer.

"Planted successfully by our inside man. The guard was easily bought - seems the Falchettis don't pay their people enough." Philo's rough laugh echoes across the empty rooftop. "The burner phone made it into Mia's hands this morning."

I pace along the roof's edge, my heels clicking against the concrete. The cool evening breeze carries the scent of the river below. "And now we wait. That foolish girl won't be able to resist trying to help her friend."

"Should we move on the apartment tonight?"

"No." I turn sharply, fixing Philo with a stern look. "We need to be patient. Let her stew in her worry first. The longer she sits with that message, the more desperate she'll become to help her friend."

Through the binoculars again, I catch movement in one of the upper windows. A slight figure pacing back and forth - Mia, no doubt, wrestling with her conscience. The same window where Enzo has been spotted keeping watch.

My jaw clenches at the thought of him. Enzo Falchetti. The way he looks at her makes my stomach turn. I've seen how he hovers, how his eyes follow her. He was never meant to protect her. She was supposed to be eliminated, another loose end tied up neatly.

"What about the younger Falchetti?" Philo asks, reading my thoughts. "He's barely left her side."

"Enzo's weakness for her will be his undoing." I run my finger along the cool metal railing. "He'll try to stop her, of course. But she'll find a way out. They always do when they think they're saving someone they love."

The sound of footsteps behind us makes me turn. Another of my men approaches, phone in hand.

"Our source inside confirms the girl accessed her voicemail twenty minutes ago." He holds out the phone, showing me the text message. "She's been visibly distressed since."

Perfect. Like a puppet on strings, dancing exactly how I want her to.

"Keep the waitress alive for now," I instruct Philo. "We may need her to make another call. And make sure the apartment is ready. I want everything in place when our little bird finally flies from her cage."

I take one last look at the mansion across the river. Behind those walls, Mia Ricci is surely pacing, her heart aching for her friend, unaware she's playing right into my hands. The Falchettis think they can protect her, but they've already lost. They just don't know it yet.

"What about the guard who helped plant the phone?" Philo asks.

"Loose ends need tying." I wave my hand dismissively. "Make it look like an accident. We can't risk him talking if the Falchettis start asking questions."

My phone buzzes - another update from inside the mansion. A smile spreads across my face as I read the message.

"She's made three attempts to leave her room in the last hour," I tell Philo. "Enzo turned her back each time. But she's growing more desperate by the minute."

I pocket my phone and gather my coat around me. The temperature has dropped with the setting sun, but the chill in the air matches the ice in my veins.

"Have the team ready to move on my command," I instruct. "When she makes her break for freedom - and she will - I want eyes on her every step of the way."

Philo nods and steps away to make the calls. I remain at the edge of the roof, watching the mansion grow darker as night falls. Somewhere inside those walls, Mia Ricci is reaching her breaking point. Soon she'll risk everything to save her friend, never realizing she's walking straight into my trap.

The city lights begin to twinkle on, reflecting off the river's dark surface. I inhale deeply, savoring the moment. Everything is falling into place. The Falchettis are about to learn what happens when they underestimate Sofia Moretti.

a daring escape
...

mia ricci

Fuck him, I thought, as I look out the window for the umpteenth time.

I press my forehead against the cool glass, watching Enzo slide into the back of the black Mercedes. His brother Dante takes the wheel while their cousin Luca claims shotgun. The tinted windows gleam in the morning sun as they pull away, tires crunching on the long gravel driveway.

Every morning, like clockwork. They leave at exactly 8:15 AM, sometimes returning for lunch, other times not appearing until well after dark. I've memorized the routine over these endless days of captivity, tracking their comings and goings from my gilded cage.

The car disappears past the iron gates, leaving me alone with my thoughts again. My fingers trace invisible patterns on the window as I replay that night in my head for the hundredth time. The heat of Enzo's skin against mine. The intensity in his eyes. The whispered promises that now feel hollow.

Since then? Radio silence. He barely looks at me when we cross paths in the halls. No explanation, no conversation, just curt nods and averted gazes. The memory of his touch burns like ice now, leaving me feeling used and discarded. Another conquest for the privileged mafia prince, I suppose.

I push away from the window, pacing the luxurious suite that's become my prison. The plush carpet muffles my frustrated footsteps as I move between the sitting area and bedroom. Everything here screams wealth - from the silk sheets to the crystal chandelier to the designer clothes they've provided. But none of it matters when I'm essentially a prisoner.

Through careful observation, I've pieced together fragments of their routine. Monday mornings usually involve meetings at their downtown offices - legitimate business fronts, I assume. Wednesdays, at the docks. Fridays bring a parade of expensive cars carrying other well-dressed men for meetings that stretch late into the night.

But Enzo remains an enigma. Sometimes he returns with blood on his knuckles. Other times, he staggers in reeking of whiskey and gunpowder. Once, I caught him staring up at my window, his expression unreadable in the darkness. But he never comes up. Never explains. Never acknowledges what happened between us.

The guards rotate shifts outside my door, a constant reminder of my captive status. Through my window, I watch the groundskeepers maintain the immaculate gardens. Maids bustle through the mansion. Life continues its carefully choreographed dance while I remain frozen in place, waiting for... what exactly?

An explanation? An apology? My freedom?

My stomach twists as I spot Giovanni's car pulling into the circular drive. Unlike his son, the Falchetti patriarch makes no effort to hide his disdain for me. His cold eyes track my every move during the mandatory family dinners, analyzing, judging, probably plotting my eventual disposal.

I sink into the window seat, drawing my knees to my chest. The mansion's grounds stretch out before me, a deceptively peaceful scene. Beyond the manicured lawns and security fences lies freedom - my old life, my independence, everything I took for granted before that fateful night at the diner.

But between here and there stands Enzo Falchetti. The man who claimed he would protect me, then locked me away and forgot about me. The man whose touch I can't forget, even as his indifference cuts deeper each day.

The Mercedes returns earlier than usual today. I watch Enzo emerge, adjusting his jacket - always impeccable, always controlled. He pauses on the steps, hand reaching into his pocket for his phone. Even from here, I can see the tension in his shoulders, the careful way he holds himself apart from everyone else.

For a moment, I think he'll look up. Acknowledge my existence in some small way. But he simply turns and follows Dante inside, leaving me to my solitude once again.

I press my palm against the glass, feeling the barrier between us. So close, yet worlds apart. The heat of my skin leaves a foggy handprint on the window - proof that I exist, that I'm more than just a problem to be managed or a witness to be contained.

A sleek black SUV pulls up to the garage, and more of their associates pile out. Another day of mysterious meetings and backroom deals while I waste away up here, caught between the woman I was and whatever I'm becoming in this twisted world of power and violence.

My hands tremble as I replay Gina's voicemail for the fifth time. Her voice, usually so bright and teasing, drips with raw terror. Each word feels like a knife twisting in my chest.

"Mia, where are you? I'm here at your place—"

I pace the plush carpet of my gilded cage, the words echoing in my head. The Falchettis may call this a guest suite, but the cameras in every corner and the guard outside my door tell a different story. Through the window, I watch the setting sun paint the manicured gardens in shades of amber and gold. Somewhere out there, Gina needs me.

The burner phone feels heavy in my palm. I slide it under my mattress, mind racing with half-formed plans. The mansion's daily routines play through my head like a movie - guards changing shifts, maids rushing through their tasks, the quiet lull that settles over the house as night approaches.

A knock at my door makes me jump. Maria bustles in, her arms full of fresh towels and sheets. My eye catches on her uniform - simple, black, practical. Perfect for blending in. As she bends to place the linens in the bathroom, I slide behind the door, my heart hammering against my ribs. When she turns to leave, I snag the spare uniform from her cart and pull it behind the door with trembling fingers.

My breath comes in short gasps as her footsteps fade down the hallway. I press my ear against the door, listening to the familiar sounds of the mansion. Rocco's heavy boots pace outside my room - fifteen steps one way, fifteen steps back. The grandfather clock in the hallway chimes seven times.

"Hey Tony," Rocco calls out, his voice gruff. "I'm dying for a smoke. Cover me for five?"

"Make it quick," Tony responds.

I press my palms against my cheeks, willing them to stop burning. "Hold on, Gina," I whisper to my reflection. "I'm coming."

* * *

MY HEART SLAMS against my ribcage so hard I fear someone might hear it echoing through the halls. The stolen maid's uniform lies sprawled across my bed, a testament to what I'm about to attempt. Maria's considerably larger frame means this could either work in my favor or be my downfall.

I grab the uniform with trembling fingers, the fabric cool against my sweaty palms. The bathroom mirror reflects my pale face as I strip off my designer clothes - another reminder of my gilded cage courtesy of the Falchetti family.

"Get it together, Mia," I whisper to myself, stepping into the uniform. The fabric hangs loose in places it shouldn't, bunching awkwardly at my waist. I tug and adjust, trying to make it look intentional rather than borrowed. The zipper catches halfway up, and I hold my breath until it finally slides home.

My fingers work through my hair, twisting it into a messy bun like I've seen Maria wear. Each piece of jewelry I remove feels like shedding another layer of myself - the delicate necklace Enzo gave me, the silver bracelet that was my mother's. I tuck them safely in my drawer, hoping I'll be back for them soon.

The uniform's hem drags slightly on the floor - Maria's got at least three inches on me. I roll the sleeves up carefully, making sure they look natural rather than adjusted. A quick glance in the mirror shows a different person staring back at me. Gone is the polished woman in expensive clothes. In her place stands someone who could pass for any of the household staff.

My hand rests on the doorknob, and I press my ear against the cool wood. The usual shuffle of Rocco's heavy boots or Tony's persistent pacing is absent. This is it - my window of opportunity.

I ease the door open, wincing at the slight creak. The hallway stretches before me, empty and silent. No sign of my guards. No sign of anyone. The Persian carpet muffles my footsteps as I step out, my body tense with anticipation.

My heartbeat thunders in my ears as I stand in the corridor. Right now, somewhere in the city, Gina needs my help. That thought steadies my trembling hands. I'm no longer just trying to escape - I'm trying to save my friend.

My fingers tremble as I adjust the starched collar, but I force my steps to remain steady, purposeful. The marble floors gleam beneath the ornate chandeliers, and I keep my eyes lowered like I've seen the other maids do.

A cluster of maids passes by, their shoes clicking against the floor. I nod politely, mumbling a quiet "good morning" while my pulse thunders in my ears. One of them smiles back, completely buying my disguise. If only they knew the truth—that I'm really their master's prisoner, desperately trying to save my friend.

"The laundry needs folding," an older maid calls out as I round the corner.

"I'll get right on it," I answer, mimicking the slight accent I've heard from the staff. The lie tastes bitter on my tongue, but Gina's frightened voice echoes in my mind, driving me forward.

The grand staircase looms ahead, its polished banister catching the light. I've memorized the guards' rotation from my days of captivity—Rocco always takes his break at this hour. Sure enough, I hear his heavy footsteps retreating, followed by the distant sound of a bathroom door closing.

My palm grows slick against the banister as I descend, each step measured and careful. The servant quarters lie just beyond, a maze of narrow corridors and storage rooms I've only glimpsed from above. A guard's voice carries from around the corner, and I freeze mid-step.

"Check the east wing again," he barks into his radio. "The boss wants extra security tonight."

I spin around, nearly colliding with another guard's broad chest. My heart stops, but muscle memory kicks in. I pivot smoothly, as if I'd meant to turn that way all along, and hurry in the opposite direction. His footsteps continue past without hesitation.

Finally reaching the servant quarters, I press myself against the cool wall, willing my racing heart to slow. The space smells of laundry detergent and floor polish, so different from the expensive perfumes and leather that permeate the upper floors. Voices drift from the break room, and I edge closer, straining to hear.

"Did you hear about the commotion at the Moretti estate?" A young maid whispers. "Three black cars rushed out last night. Something big is happening."

"Keep your voice down," another responds. "You know we're not supposed to discuss family business."

My fingers curl into fists. Whatever the Morettis are planning, Gina's caught in the middle of it. I scan the corridor, noting the staff entrance at the far end. If I can just make it there without being spotted...

A key ring hangs on a hook near the time clock, labeled "**Delivery Van 2.**" My breath catches. A potential escape route, if I'm brave enough—or desperate enough—to take it.

the unraveling
. . .

mia ricci

The stolen van's engine purrs to life under my trembling hands. I've never stolen anything before - not even a candy bar - but here I am, about to drive off with the Falchetti's delivery vehicle. My heart hammers against my ribs as I ease the van forward, praying none of the guards notice.

"Come on, come on," I whisper, willing my shaking fingers to cooperate as I navigate through the service entrance. The steering wheel feels slick under my sweaty palms.

I hold my breath until I clear the gates, half-expecting alarms to blare or guards to come running. But nothing happens. I'm actually doing this. I'm escaping.

My eyes dart constantly to the rearview mirror as I weave through the city streets. Every black SUV makes my stomach lurch. Every motorcycle revving behind me sends my pulse racing. Gina needs me though. That voicemail... the raw fear in her voice... I have to get to her.

I take random turns, doubling back occasionally to ensure I'm not being followed. The stolen maid's uniform itches against my skin, a constant reminder of what I've done. What will Enzo think when he discovers I'm gone? The thought sends an unexpected pang through my chest.

The farther I drive from the Falchetti mansion, the tighter my chest feels. Images of Enzo's face flash through my mind - how those intense eyes will darken with fury when he discovers I'm gone. I've seen his temper before, the way his jaw clenches and his shoulders go rigid when he's angry. But this... *this* will be different.

"He's gonna fucking lose it," I mutter, gripping the steering wheel tighter. The thought of Enzo unleashing that carefully controlled rage makes me shiver. Not just because I betrayed his protection, but because I violated his trust. After everything that's happened between us - that night we shared, the growing tension, those moments when his guard slips and I glimpse something softer beneath his tough exterior...

A horn blares, snapping me back to attention. I've drifted too close to the yellow line. *Focus, Mia.* I can't let thoughts of Enzo distract me. But it's like trying not to think about a splinter under your skin - the more you try to ignore it, the more it nags at you.

The van feels emptier somehow, colder. I miss the weight of his presence, even when he was driving me crazy with his overprotective hovering. Miss how he'd appear in doorways to check on me, his broad shoulders filling the frame. Miss those rare half-smiles that would crack his stern expression when I managed to surprise him.

"Stop it," I tell myself firmly. "You're doing this for Gina." But the words sound hollow in the quiet van.

Each mile marker feels like another wall going up between us. The city lights blur past my windows as my mind wanders to all the what-ifs. *What if I never see him again?* The thought hits harder than expected, leaving an ache in my chest I can't explain. We're from different worlds - his ruled by power and violence, mine... well, mine used to be simple before I witnessed that shooting.

My fingers drum restlessly on the wheel as I remember how safe I felt with him, despite everything. How he'd position himself between me and any perceived threat. The gentle way he'd touch my arm to guide me, so at odds with his dangerous reputation.

Traffic thickens as I enter downtown, forcing me to slow down. In the stop-and-go rhythm, my thoughts spiral deeper. *Will he come after me himself? Send his men? Or will he write me off as not worth the trouble?* That last possibility shouldn't hurt as much as it does.

A police car cruises past and my heart leaps into my throat. But it continues on, oblivious to the stolen van and the fugitive waitress behind the wheel. I release a shaky breath. The uniform suddenly feels like it's strangling me, and I tug at the collar.

"You're doing the right thing," I whisper, but my voice wavers. The memory of Enzo's warmth beside me on those nights when neither of us could sleep, just talking in low voices about nothing important, hits me like a physical blow. The way he'd lean in slightly when I spoke, actually listening. How his fingers would sometimes brush mine, sending electricity through my skin.

I blink hard, forcing back tears I didn't expect. This isn't about Enzo. This is about saving my friend. But even as I think it, I know I'm lying to myself. Everything's about Enzo now - has been since that first night together, long before I witnessed the shooting that threw us back into each other's orbit.

The streets grow more familiar as I near my neighborhood. But instead of feeling relieved, each block brings a heavier weight of uncertainty. I'm choosing my old life over whatever was building between Enzo and me. The right choice, the safe choice - so why does it feel like I'm making a terrible mistake?

My hands tremble slightly on the wheel as I picture the betrayal that will flash in those dark eyes when he realizes what I've done. The wall will come slamming back up, harder than ever. Any progress we've made, any trust we've built - gone in an instant.

Finally, my apartment building comes into view - a shabby five-story walk-up that's never looked more beautiful. I park the van haphazardly, probably blocking someone's spot, but I don't care. My legs are shaking so badly I nearly stumble getting out.

"Please be okay, please be okay," I mutter as I rush inside, taking the stairs two at a time. The familiar smell of musty carpet and old cigarettes hits me as I reach my floor. Home. Safety.

I fumble with my keys, grateful I had them in my pocket when the Falchettis took me. The lock clicks and I burst inside.

"Gina?" My voice echoes in the darkness. Something feels wrong. The air is too still, too quiet. "Gina, are you here?"

The hairs on the back of my neck stand up just as the door slams shut behind me with a thunderous bang. Before I can scream, the lights flick on.

Sofia Moretti stands in my living room, looking like death wrapped in designer clothing. Her blood-red lips curve into a predatory smile as four men in black suits materialize from the shadows, boxing me in.

"Ms. Ricci," Sofia purrs, her voice like honey laced with poison. "How kind of you to finally join us." She gestures to one of her men, who moves to block the door. "I must say, I'm impressed. Stealing a delivery van? Who knew our little waitress had such... initiative."

My throat closes up as the reality of my situation hits me. There is no Gina. There never was. I've walked straight into their trap like a complete idiot.

"Where's Gina?" I demand anyway, my voice barely above a whisper.

Sofia's smile widens, showing perfect white teeth. "Your friend Gina? She's perfectly fine." Her heels click against my hardwood floor as she approaches. "In fact, she's probably serving coffee at that charming little diner right now, counting the generous bonus I gave her."

My stomach drops. "What?"

"Come now, Ms. Ricci. Did you really think someone struggling to make rent and drowning in car payments wouldn't jump at an opportunity to earn some quick cash?" Sofia's expensive perfume chokes me as she circles closer. "All it took was a few thousand dollars to clear her debts and cover her expenses for the next six months. Your dear friend practically leaped at the chance to help us."

The betrayal hits me like a physical blow. Gina and I have worked together for over a year. We've shared lunches, swapped shifts, complained about difficult customers. I thought we were friends. "You're lying."

"Am I?" Sofia pulls out her phone, tapping the screen before holding it up. A video plays - Gina sitting in what looks like a fancy restaurant, nervously accepting an envelope from one of

Sofia's men. "She didn't even hesitate when we explained what we needed. Just asked how many times she should call your voicemail."

My legs feel weak. All those conversations we've had, all those times I confided in her about my parents, about my dreams of becoming a writer, about that night with Enzo... was any of it real? Or was she just collecting information, waiting for the right buyer?

"The fear in her voice was quite convincing, wasn't it?" Sofia continues, clearly enjoying my distress. "We didn't even need any special equipment. Your trusted friend did all the acting herself. Though I must say, she was rather concerned about whether this would get you hurt." She laughs softly. "Don't worry, I assured her we just wanted to talk."

I think about all the times Gina listened to me vent about feeling trapped working at the diner; how I wished I could write a best seller. How she always seemed so sympathetic, encouraging me to stay strong. Was she reporting everything back to Sofia? The thought makes me sick.

"Of course, she did ask what would happen if you didn't come," Sofia adds, examining her perfectly manicured nails. "Such a practical girl, your Gina. Once I explained that the money would clear regardless, she seemed much more comfortable with the arrangement."

The room spins slightly. Every shared laugh, every comforting hug, every secret whispered during slow shifts - all of it feels tainted now. How long has Gina been working for Sofia? Was anything about our friendship real?

"You look surprised," Sofia observes, her voice dripping with false concern. "Did you really believe a struggling waitress would choose loyalty over financial security? That's adorably naive." She steps even closer, her designer perfume making my eyes water. "Everyone has a price, Ms. Ricci. Your friend's was simply lower than most."

My chest feels tight, like I can't get enough air. I trusted Gina. Confided in her. And all this time, she was just waiting for the highest bidder. I think about her sympathetic smiles when I talked about missing my parents, her encouraging words when I shared my writing dreams. Was she cataloging my weaknesses, looking for vulnerabilities to exploit?

"If it makes you feel any better," Sofia continues, "she did seem genuinely fond of you. Called you sweet, caring - said you didn't deserve to be caught up in all this." Her smile turns cruel. "But I suppose even friendship has its limits when there's enough money on the table."

The worst part is, I can't even blame Gina entirely. How many times had she mentioned struggling with her car payments? How often did she worry about making rent? I'd been too caught up in my own problems to really notice, but Sofia had been paying attention. Had seen the desperation and known exactly how to exploit it.

"You manipulated her," I say, but my voice sounds weak even to my own ears.

* * *

I STAND FROZEN as Sofia circles me like a predator, her dark eyes gleaming with a hatred that makes my blood run cold. The soldiers block every escape route, their weapons trained on me, a stark reminder that I walked straight into their trap.

"Look at you." Sofia's lips curl into a sneer. "The little waitress who thinks she can play in our world." Her heels click against the hardwood floor of my apartment, each step making me flinch. "Do you have any idea how long I've waited to get back at the Falchettis? How many nights I've planned this?"

My mouth goes dry. "I don't understand. I haven't done anything to you—"

"Shut up!" She whirls on me, her composure cracking. "My father built an empire from nothing. And what did the Falchettis do? They stole millions from us, piece by piece, deal by deal. Then they had the audacity to kill my cousin Tony at that pathetic diner of yours."

The memory of that night floods back - the gunshots, the blood, the chaos. "I didn't know he was your cousin. I just saw—"

"You saw exactly what they wanted you to see." Sofia's voice drips with venom. "And now you're living in their mansion, protected by their precious Enzo like some kind of pet."

I shake my head, desperate to make her understand. "Please, I'm not part of their world. I'm just a waitress who was in the wrong place at the wrong time. I don't want any part of this feud."

"You think I care what you want?" She laughs, the sound sharp and cruel. "You became part of this the moment you witnessed Tony's murder. And now?" Her eyes narrow. "Now you're exactly what I need."

My heart pounds against my ribs. "I won't help you hurt anyone."

"You already are, just by existing." Sofia moves closer, her perfume suffocating me. "Enzo's grown soft, protecting you. The mighty Falchetti enforcer, playing bodyguard to a nobody." Her fingers grip my chin, forcing me to look at her. "Tell me, does he whisper sweet nothings in your ear? Make you feel special?"

I try to pull away, but her grip tightens. "You're wrong about him."

"No, you're wrong if you think he *actually* cares. Men like Enzo only understand power and revenge." She releases me with a sharp push. "And he's going to come running when he realizes his little bird has flown the cage."

The reality of her words hits me like a physical blow. "You're using me as bait?"

"Finally, she gets it." Sofia's smile turns predatory. "But it's more than that. The Falchettis took everything from us - our money, our respect, our family. Now?" Her eyes flash with malice. "Now I'm going to watch Enzo suffer before I end him. And you're going to help me do it."

"I won't—"

"You don't have a choice." She cuts me off, her voice hard as steel. "You're just a pawn in a game that started long before you stumbled into it. The Falchettis need to pay for what they've done, and Enzo's death will just be the beginning."

I feel the walls closing in, the weight of years of hatred and violence pressing down on me. This isn't about me anymore - it never was. I'm just collateral damage in a war I never knew existed.

"Your father's money," I try one last time, "surely there's another way—"

"This stopped being about money the moment they killed Tony." Sofia's face contorts with rage. "This is about making them feel what I felt. And you, my dear?" She reaches out to brush a strand of hair from my face, making me recoil. "You're going to help me break Enzo Falchetti into pieces."

discovery
...

enzo falchetti

𝒯he iron gates groan open as I pull my Mercedes through them, gravel crunching beneath the tires. Home. Finally. After three days of back-to-back meetings with our business associates, pretending to care about profit margins and distribution channels, all I can think about is seeing her again.

Mia.

My fingers drum against the steering wheel as the mansion comes into view, its stone facade glowing amber in the late afternoon sun. I've tried so hard to maintain my distance, to act like she doesn't affect me. Like I don't notice the way her eyes light up when she laughs, or how she bites her lower lip when she's deep in thought.

But she's gotten under my skin. These past few days away have been torture, knowing she's here, in my home, so close yet untouchable. The memory of our one night together still burns hot in my mind, making it impossible to focus on anything else.

I park in front of the grand entrance, tossing my keys to Marco, our longtime valet. "Welcome back, Mr. Falchetti." His tone seems off, almost hesitant.

The massive double doors swing open as I climb the steps, my footsteps echoing through the marble foyer. Something feels... different. The usual bustling energy of the house seems charged with an unfamiliar tension.

Maria, one of our maids, scurries past me with her head bowed low. She nearly drops her cleaning supplies trying to curtsy. "Mr. Falchetti," she mumbles, not meeting my eyes.

What the fuck?

I continue down the main hallway, and the whispers start. They drift from corners and doorways, hushed voices falling silent as I pass. Two security guards exchange meaningful looks. A butler practically jumps out of my way.

My stomach knots. Years of living in this world have taught me to trust my instincts, and right now, they're screaming that something's wrong.

"She just... disappeared," I catch fragments of conversation from the kitchen staff. "Right under their noses..."

"Quiet!" someone hisses. "He's back."

I stop dead in my tracks. *She?* My blood runs cold.

The excitement that had been building in my chest curdles into dread. I quicken my pace, taking the stairs two at a time toward the guest wing. Toward Mia's room.

Discovery

Rocco stands outside her door, but his usual stoic expression is replaced with barely concealed panic. He straightens when he sees me, sweat beading on his forehead.

"Mr. Falchetti, I—"

I shoulder past him, throwing open the door. The room is empty. The bed is made, everything in its place, but it feels wrong. Dead. Like a museum piece rather than a lived-in space.

"Where is she?" My voice comes out low, dangerous.

Rocco shifts his weight. "Sir, I only stepped away for a minute—"

"WHERE IS SHE?" The words explode from my chest, echoing off the walls.

"We... we don't know, sir. She managed to get past security somehow. Disguised herself as one of the maids. We've got teams searching the grounds, but..."

The rage builds inside me like a gathering storm. My fists clench at my sides as I take in the abandoned room. All those careful walls I built, all that practiced indifference - it crumbles away, leaving only fear and fury in its wake.

She's gone. Mia's gone. Out there somewhere in a city crawling with Moretti soldiers who'd love nothing more than to get their hands on her. And it's my fault. I let my guard down, let myself believe she was safe here.

"How long?" I demand through gritted teeth.

"We discovered her missing about two hours ago—"

"Two hours?" I whirl on him. "She's been gone for two fucking hours and I'm just finding out now?"

The color drains from Rocco's face. "Your father ordered us not to contact you during your meetings-"

Of course, he did. My father, always trying to maintain control, even when everything's falling apart. But he doesn't understand. He doesn't know what the Morettis are capable of, what they'll do to her if they find her first.

Every second we waste is another second she could be in danger.

"You had *one* job." My fingers curl into fists at my sides. "One *fucking* job. To watch her. To keep her safe."

The weight of failure crashes down on my shoulders. I trusted him to guard her, to protect what's mine—what's under my protection. The correction comes too late, even in my own mind.

"Sofia Moretti has her."

The words hit like a physical blow. My stomach drops, and for a moment, the elegant hallway spins around me. Sofia. That calculating bitch who's been gunning for our family for years. Who'd do anything to hurt us.

To hurt *me*.

"Get the cars ready." My voice comes out rough. "I want every available man—"

"Going in guns blazing won't help anyone." Dante's cool voice cuts through my racing thoughts. My brother materializes from the shadows, blocking my path with his broad frame. "Think this through, little brother."

"Get out of my way."

"She was always a loose end." Dante's dark eyes bore into mine. "You knew that from the start. This is what happens when we let emotions cloud our judgment."

"A loose end?" I bark out a harsh laugh. "That's rich, coming from you. If she was such a liability, why did we protect her? Why didn't we just eliminate the threat like we usually do?"

Dante's jaw tightens. "Because you insisted—"

"No." I step closer, getting in his face. "Because Father agreed. Because somewhere along the line, we all recognized that she deserved better than to be another casualty in this war. And now you want to what? Leave her to Sofia's mercy?"

"I want you to think like a Falchetti." Dante's voice drops lower, deadlier. "Not like some lovesick fool rushing to his death."

"Think like a Falchetti?" The words taste bitter on my tongue. "You mean abandon someone who trusted us? Someone whose only crime was being in the wrong place at the wrong time?"

My heart pounds harder, memories of Mia's smile flashing through my mind. Her gentle touch. The way she looked at me like I could be more than just another monster in this family of killers.

"She's bait." Dante grabs my arm. "Sofia's using her to draw you out. To make you react exactly like this."

"I don't care." I wrench free of his grip. "If Sofia wants me, she can have me. But I'm not letting Mia pay the price for our family's sins."

"Our family's sins?" Dante's eyes narrow dangerously. "You mean our family's survival? Our strength? Everything Father built—"

"Everything Father built is meaningless if we can't protect innocent people caught in the crossfire." The words explode from me, echoing off the mansion's walls.

* * *

I SLAM the library door behind me, my hands trembling with rage. The dark wood paneling and leather-bound books blur together as I pace the length of the room. My footsteps echo against the hardwood floors, matching the pounding in my chest.

"Fuck!" I drive my fist into the nearest bookshelf. Pain shoots through my knuckles, but it doesn't come close to the agony tearing through my chest at the thought of Mia in Sofia's hands.

The crystal decanter of whiskey catches my eye. I pour myself two fingers, but the glass shakes in my grip. The amber liquid sloshes over the rim as memories of Mia flood my mind - her smile at the diner, the way she challenged me even when scared, how soft her skin felt under my touch that one night...

A gentle knock breaks through my spiral. Lila stands in the doorway, her red hair catching the late afternoon light. The concern in her eyes reminds me of how she looked when Dante first brought her here - another innocent caught in our violent world.

"Your brother told me what happened," she says, closing the door behind her. "About Mia."

"Save the lecture." I knock back the whiskey. "I've already heard it from Dante."

"I'm not here to lecture you." Lila moves closer, her steps careful but determined. "I'm here because I remember what it was like - being the outsider, the liability everyone wanted to eliminate."

The truth in her words hits harder than the alcohol. "This is different. Sofia has her."

"Which is exactly why she needs you fighting for her, not hiding in here drowning your guilt."

"You don't understand what Sofia's capable of—"

"No, but I understand what it's like to have your entire world turned upside down." Lila's gaze pins me in place. "And I see the way you look at her, Enzo. The same way Dante looked at me when he decided I was worth protecting."

My grip tightens on the empty glass. "What are you asking?"

"Do you have feelings for Mia?"

The question hangs between us. I close my eyes, seeing Mia's face - not just her beauty, but her strength, her kindness, the fire in her that refuses to be extinguished even in the darkest moments.

I run my hand through my hair, pacing again as Lila's question echoes in my mind. Of course, she noticed - she's always been observant, which is probably why Dante fell for her in the first place. Every shared glance with Mia during that tense family dinner felt like a jolt of electricity through my veins.

"You saw right through me at dinner, didn't you?" The words come out rougher than intended.

Lila's lips curve into a knowing smile. "It wasn't exactly subtle. Every time she looked up from her plate, your entire body language changed. The way you positioned yourself between her and Giovanni, how your jaw clenched whenever someone directed a question at her..."

I drain another glass of whiskey, letting the burn distract me from the truth in Lila's words. But the memories flood in anyway - Mia's delicate fingers wrapped around her wine glass, the slight tremble in her voice that made me want to reach across the table and take her hand, the quiet strength in her eyes when she answered my father's probing questions.

"Christ." I set the glass down hard enough to make it crack. "What the hell is happening to me?"

"You're falling for her," Lila states it like it's the most natural thing in the world, not a catastrophic complication in an already dangerous situation.

"I can't—" The words stick in my throat. "This isn't some romance novel, Lila. Sofia will tear her apart just to get to me, to get to all of us."

"And yet every time Mia so much as breathes in your direction, you look at her like she's the answer to questions you didn't even know you were asking."

Her words hit too close to home. I think about dinner again - how my heart stopped when Mia accidentally brushed against me reaching for the salt, how I had to grip my knife to keep from touching her back. The way her scent - something soft and floral - made me want to bury my face in her neck right there at the family table.

"You don't understand." I drag my hands down my face. "Every protective instinct I have goes haywire around her. During dinner, when father started questioning her about the diner incident - I wanted to grab her and run. Just get her away from all of this."

"That's not just protection, Enzo."

"Then what is it?" The question comes out more desperate than I intended. "Because I've never felt this... this out of control. This consumed. She looks at me and I forget everything - who I am, what I've done, the blood on my hands."

Lila steps closer, her expression softening. "That's called falling in love."

The words hit me like a physical blow. *Love?* The concept seems absurd in our world of violence and betrayal. And yet... I think of Mia's smile, how it lights up her whole face. How she maintains her kindness despite being thrown into this nightmare. The way she challenges me, refuses to be cowed even when surrounded by killers.

"Every time she looked up at dinner," I admit, my voice barely above a whisper, "all I wanted was to wrap my arms around her. Keep her safe. Make her understand that she's not alone in this."

"And that terrifies you."

"Of course it fucking terrifies me!" I spin away from Lila's knowing look. "I'm supposed to be her protector, not... not whatever this is becoming. I can't afford to feel this way. She can't afford for me to feel this way."

The weight of it all crashes down on me. Every stolen glance at dinner, every suppressed urge to touch her, to comfort her - it's all evidence of something I can't control, something that could get us both killed. My feelings for Mia are becoming a liability that Sofia will exploit without mercy.

the reckoning
...

enzo falchetti

I pace the length of my father's study like a caged animal, my footsteps echoing off the mahogany panels. Each second that ticks by is another moment Mia spends in Sofia's clutches. My hands clench and unclench, itching for action, for violence, for anything other than this helpless waiting.

"Any word?" I bark into my phone for the hundredth time. Another dead end from our street contacts. I hurl the device across the room, watching it bounce off the leather sofa.

The weight in my chest grows heavier with each passing minute. I should have spent more time with her, should have seen the signs of her restlessness. Instead, I kept my distance, trying to deny the pull between us. Now all I can think about is her smile, the way her eyes lit up when she talked about her dreams of becoming a writer, how she managed to stay kind despite everything we put her through.

My stomach turns as images of Sofia's previous victims flash through my mind. I've seen her handiwork firsthand - the creative ways she extracts information and revenge. The thought of those same methods being used on Mia makes bile rise in my throat. Sofia's cousin Tony deserved what he got, but Mia? She's innocent in all this. Just a waitress who was in the wrong place at the wrong time.

"An eye for an eye," I mutter, remembering Sofia's favorite saying. The bitch is probably enjoying every second of this, knowing how it's tearing me apart. She'll want to make Mia suffer just like she believes her cousin suffered.

I can't take it anymore. This waiting, this uselessness - it's suffocating me. My feet carry me down to the underground parking garage, the fluorescent lights casting harsh shadows across the concrete. My Ducati sits there, sleek and black, promising speed and freedom.

I run my hand along the smooth metal of the gas tank. The key feels heavy in my pocket. I know every route Sofia might take, every safehouse she could be using. The smart play is to wait for intel, to move with backup. But standing here, staring at my bike, all I can think about is Mia's face that last morning - how she looked at me like I might actually be worth something more than my family name.

The garage feels too small, too constricting. The walls seem to close in as my mind races through possibilities, each worse than the last. My fingertips trace the Ducati's handlebars, remembering all the times this bike has been my escape. But this isn't about escape anymore. It's about bringing her home.

My chest constricts as I imagine what Sofia might be doing to her right now. The Moretti princess always did have a talent for psychological torture - she knows how to break people in ways that leave no visible scars. And Mia, with her gentle heart and quiet strength, doesn't deserve any of this nightmare.

I grip the handlebars tighter, my knuckles turning white. The garage's ventilation system hums overhead, a monotonous drone that matches the buzzing in my head. Every minute I waste here is another minute Sofia has to destroy everything good and pure about Mia. Another minute where I'm failing the one person who saw past my carefully constructed walls.

The weight of my gun presses against my lower back, a constant reminder of who I am and what I'm capable of. I've never hesitated to pull the trigger before - it's part of being a Falchetti. But now, with Mia's life hanging in the balance, the stakes feel different. Personal in a way that makes my hands shake.

I rev my motorcycle's engine, letting the familiar rumble vibrate through my body as I stand at the edge of our family's estate. A smirk plays across my lips, imagining Dante's face when he realizes I've gone against his direct orders. The thought of Mia in Sofia's clutches tears at my chest, overriding any lingering doubt about defying the family.

"Fuck loyalty," I mutter, kickstarting the bike. The wind whips against my face as I tear down the winding driveway, leaving behind everything I've ever known. Mia's face flashes in my mind - her delicate features, those expressive brown eyes that haunted me since our first night together. The image of her trapped, terrified, makes my hands grip the handlebars tighter.

I weave through the city streets, my mind racing through possible locations. Sofia's not stupid enough to take Mia somewhere obvious. Then it hits me - the abandoned warehouse on Tenth. That shithole where the Morettis conduct their dirtiest business. The perfect place to hold someone captive.

The warehouse looms ahead, its decrepit structure casting long shadows in the fading light. I slow down, scanning the perimeter. Five of Sofia's men lounging outside, trying to look casual but their posture screams 'guard dogs.' Their hands rest too close to their concealed weapons, eyes constantly scanning the streets.

My heart pounds against my ribs as I assess the situation. There's no way I'm getting past them without creating a scene. A reckless plan forms in my mind - the kind that would make even Dante question my sanity. But for Mia? Worth it.

I gun the engine, aiming straight for the group. Their heads snap up at the sound, hands reaching for weapons. At the last second, I lay the bike down, letting it crash and slide across the concrete. The screech of metal on pavement pierces the air.

"Hey assholes!" I push myself up, spreading my arms wide. "You want a Falchetti? Here's your fucking chance!"

The first shots ring out before I finish speaking. I dive behind a dumpster, my breath coming in sharp bursts. Footsteps thunder closer as Sofia's men advance. A bullet pings off the metal near my head.

"Come out, little prince!" One of them taunts. "Sofia's been waiting for you."

I take a deep breath, preparing to make my move. But as I shift my weight, ready to bolt, rough hands grab my shoulders. Two more of Sofia's men materialize behind me - the backup I should have anticipated. Their grip is bruising as they wrench my arms behind my back.

"Not so tough now, are you?" One sneers, pressing the barrel of his gun against my temple.

I struggle against their hold, but it's useless. Five more men surround me, their weapons trained on my chest. I force myself to go still, knowing this captured prey act is exactly what I needed. Because where they take me, they'll take me to Mia.

"Take him to Sofia," the leader barks. "She's gonna want to deal with this one personally."

They drag me toward the warehouse entrance, my feet scraping against concrete. Blood trickles down my temple from the crash, but I barely notice the pain. My entire focus narrows to one thought: *I'm coming for you, Mia. Just hold on.*

* * *

I SLAM against the concrete floor, pain shooting through my shoulder as Sofia's men toss me into the dark room like a sack of garbage. The metallic taste of blood lingers in my mouth from where they'd struck me earlier. Doesn't matter. None of it matters when I spot her.

Mia.

She's huddled in the corner, wrists bound behind her back, but alive. *Thank God she's alive.* My chest loosens just enough to breathe again. The terror in her eyes pierces straight through me, but there's something else there too - a stubborn defiance that makes my heart clench.

"Well, well." Sofia's voice drips with satisfaction as she circles outside our makeshift prison. "The mighty Enzo Falchetti, throwing himself right into my lap. How thoughtful of you."

I push myself to my knees, ignoring the throb in my shoulder. "Let her go, Sofia. She has nothing to do with this."

"Oh, but she does now." Sofia's heels click against the floor as she paces. "She became everything the moment your family decided to kill my cousin Tony. An eye for an eye, wouldn't you say?"

"Your cousin was dealing on our territory," I spit out. "He knew the consequences."

Sofia's laugh echoes off the walls. "Always so righteous, aren't you? Just like your brother." She stops pacing, her shadow falling across us. "You thought you could protect her? Poor, sweet Enzo. This is *my* city now. Your family? They're nothing but relics of the past."

I catch Mia's gaze across the room, trying to convey everything I can't say out loud. *That I'm sorry. That I'll get her out of this.* Her chin lifts slightly - the tiniest nod of understanding that makes my chest tighten.

"You won't get away with this," I growl, but Sofia just smirks.

"I already have. Your father's empire is crumbling, Enzo. And now I have his precious son and this... liability." She gestures dismissively at Mia. "Perhaps I'll let you watch what happens to people who cross the Moretti family before I deal with you."

My muscles coil with rage, straining against the zip ties cutting into my wrists. "Touch her and I'll—"

"You'll what?" Sofia's voice turns sharp as a blade. "You're in no position to make threats. Look at you - throwing everything away for some waitress. Your family name, your legacy, all of it. Pathetic."

I force myself to stay still, to think past the fury clouding my judgment. One wrong move and Mia pays the price. Sofia continues her taunting, but I tune her out, focused on finding a way - any way - to get us both out alive.

"This is my city," Sofia declares again, her victorious smile visible through the bars. "And your family is nothing!"

The Reckoning

I say nothing, letting her believe she's won. Let her gloat and strut. But my mind is already racing, cataloging every detail of our prison, every guard's position, every possible advantage we might have. I refuse to let this be how our story ends.

Mia shifts slightly in her corner, and our eyes meet again. The fear is still there, but something else too - trust. She trusts me, despite everything. Despite my family, despite the danger I've brought into her life. It hits me like a physical blow, that quiet faith in her eyes.

I've never wanted to be worthy of someone's trust more in my life.

tension in the air
...

mia ricci

I can't tear my gaze away from Enzo's bruised face, his split lip, the blood trickling down his temple. All because of me. My stupid, impulsive decision to run. To try to save Gina, who wasn't even in danger. The guilt sits like lead in my stomach.

Sofia's men really worked him over when they brought him in. The memory of his body hitting the concrete floor makes me wince. Yet here he is, still positioning himself between me and the door, still trying to protect me even though we're both trapped in this hellhole.

"I'm sorry," I whisper, my voice cracking. "This is all my fault. If I hadn't—"

Enzo shakes his head, cutting me off. Even now, he won't let me shoulder the blame. *But how can I not?* My reckless escape attempt brought the youngest Falchetti heir right into Sofia's hands. God knows how many more people will die because of what I set in motion.

A sudden bang from outside makes us both snap our heads up toward the small, grimy window near the ceiling. The sound echoes through our makeshift cell, making my heart skip several beats. Another crash follows, closer this time.

I look at Enzo, questions burning on my tongue. His eyes meet mine, and he gives me a subtle nod. That simple gesture sends hope and terror coursing through my veins in equal measure. Help might be coming - but what if it's not? What if it's just Sofia's men coming to finish what they started?

My hands start trembling as I pull my knees closer to my chest. The zip ties around my wrists dig into my skin, but I barely notice the pain. All I can focus on is the growing chaos outside. The unknown lurking behind that door terrifies me more than Sofia's cold smile ever did.

Metal scrapes against metal somewhere in the warehouse. Footsteps thunder overhead. A man shouts something I can't quite make out, his voice muffled by distance and walls.

"Enzo," I breathe, hating how small and frightened my voice sounds. He inches closer to me, his shoulder brushing mine. The contact steadies me somewhat, but my heart still races wildly in my chest.

The warehouse doors rattle violently, the sound amplified in our concrete prison. More shouting now, multiple voices. The crack of gunfire makes me jump, a small cry escaping my lips before I can stop it.

Enzo presses closer, his warmth a shield against the terror threatening to overwhelm me. I want to close my eyes, to shut out whatever's coming, but I force myself to keep them open. If these are my final moments, I won't face them like a coward.

The door to our cell groans under some unseen pressure. Once, twice. The third impact sends vibrations through the floor beneath us. I grip Enzo's arm, my fingers digging into his sleeve as the noise outside grows to a deafening crescendo.

"Stay behind me," he murmurs, the first words he's spoken since they threw him in here. The command in his voice brooks no argument, even now.

Another explosion of sound rocks the warehouse. Closer now, much closer. The walls seem to shake with each impact. My ears ring with the myriad of shouts, gunfire, and what sounds like splintering wood.

The warehouse echoes with sudden shouts and thuds, making me jump. My heart pounds against my ribs as the sounds of fighting grow louder outside. Through the grimy windows, shadows dance and clash in the dim light.

Enzo's shoulders tense beside me. His jaw clenches as he tilts his head, listening intently. I know what he's thinking - the Falchetti men must have found us. The thought brings both relief and fresh terror. Who knows what Sofia might do now that she's cornered?

Sofia's heels click sharply against the concrete floor as she strides toward one of her men. "Check it out," she snaps, her voice tight with barely contained anger. "Deal with whoever's out there." The thug nods and hurries away, leaving Sofia to pace like a caged tiger, her perfectly manicured nails drumming against her crossed arms.

When Sofia finally stalks out after her man, the warehouse falls into an eerie silence. The ropes bite into my wrists as I shift uncomfortably. The quiet feels almost worse than the chaos - at least then I knew what was happening.

I turn to look at Enzo, guilt crushing my chest. His face is streaked with dirt and blood from the earlier struggle, and it's all my fault. "I'm *so* sorry this happened," I whisper, my voice cracking. "I never wanted to drag you into this."

Enzo's hands find mine despite our restraints, his grip warm and reassuring. His eyes lock onto mine with an intensity that makes my breath catch. "You don't understand, Mia. I love you." A crooked smile plays at his lips. "Will you marry me?"

I gape at him, wondering if he's lost his mind. "Enzo, this is insane!" The words burst out before I can stop them. "We could die here! You can't be serious!" My pulse races wildly, torn between the absurdity of the moment and the way my heart leaps at his words.

Looking down at our joined hands, I take a shaky breath. "I can't say yes to that... not when we're in this mess." The words taste bitter on my tongue. I catch the glimmer of humor in his eyes - he's trying to lighten the mood, I know - but there's something else there too, something real that makes my chest ache.

* * *

THE SHOUTS OUTSIDE GROW LOUDER, gunfire popping in quick bursts that make me flinch. My heart pounds against my ribs as I strain to hear what's happening beyond these warehouse walls. *Are those really Falchetti men out there, coming to save us? Or is it someone worse?*

I glance at Enzo beside me, his proposal still echoing in my head. The ropes bite into my wrists as I shift position, trying to find some comfort on the cold concrete floor. "Do you think it's your brother?"

"Could be." Enzo's voice is tight with tension. His shoulders flex against his restraints, testing them for any give. "Or it could be the Moretti's backup arriving."

A scream pierces the air, followed by the sickening crunch of metal on metal. I squeeze my eyes shut, willing myself not to imagine what's happening out there. The violence of this world still feels foreign to me, like a nightmare I can't wake up from.

"I don't want to die here." The words slip out before I can stop them, small and broken in the dim light. "Not like this. Not tied up in some warehouse because I saw something I shouldn't have."

"Look at me." Enzo's command cuts through my rising panic. When I meet his gaze, his dark eyes burn with intensity. "You're not going to die here. I won't let that happen."

But he's as trapped as I am, and his promises, however fierce, can't change that reality. The ropes around my wrists are proof enough. More gunfire erupts, closer now. The walls seem to vibrate with each shot.

"Why did you really propose to me?" I ask, needing a distraction from the chaos outside. "Was it just because you thought we were going to die?"

A muscle ticks in Enzo's jaw. "I meant what I said. Every word."

"You barely know me."

"I know enough." His voice drops lower, rougher. "I know you're brave. I know you see the good in people, even when they don't deserve it. I know you make me want to be better than what this life has made me."

My chest aches at his words, but the sound of running footsteps interrupts whatever response I might have given. Heavy boots thunder down the hallway outside our prison. I hold my breath, terror clawing up my throat.

The footsteps stop. Someone shouts orders in Italian - the words too fast for me to catch. More boots, more voices.

"If that's Sofia's men..." I whisper, unable to finish the thought.

"Then we fight." Enzo shifts closer to me, his shoulder pressing against mine. The warmth of him is reassuring, even now. "Whatever happens, we fight."

The door handle rattles. Metal scrapes against metal. My heart stutters, then races. This is it. Either salvation or execution waits on the other side of that door.

I think of my quiet life before all this - serving coffee, dreaming of writing romance novels, living in blessed ignorance of the darkness that ran beneath the city's surface. How naive I was. How unprepared for the reality of falling into this world of violence and passion.

The lock clicks. I grab Enzo's hand, ignoring the awkward angle of our bound wrists. His fingers intertwine with mine, squeezing tight. If these are my last moments, at least I'm not alone.

The door swings open with a rusty screech. Light floods in, momentarily blinding me. I blink rapidly, trying to make out the figures in the doorway. *Are they friends or enemies? Saviors or executioners?*

More footsteps approach from behind whoever stands in the doorway. The tension in the air is thick enough to choke on. I grip Enzo's hand tighter, my palm sweaty against his.

"If we get out of this," I whisper, the words tumbling out in a rush, "ask me again. About marriage. Ask me when we're not tied up in a warehouse with guns pointed at us. Ask me when I can actually believe we have a future."

My heart nearly stops as the door flies open, crashing against the wall. Sofia's heels click against the concrete floor, each step echoing like a death knell. Her ruby-red lips curve into a smile that sends ice through my veins. The warehouse lights cast harsh shadows across her face, making her look more demon than human.

She fixes those dark eyes on Enzo, and I feel him tense beside me. "Oh, Enzo, how sweet." Her voice drips with false sweetness. "Your bride won't see tomorrow. Such a romantic fool you are." The words slice through the air between us.

I watch Enzo's jaw clench, the muscles in his neck straining against his skin. His eyes burn with a fury I've never seen before. "You won't get away with this," he snarls, and despite our bonds, I feel the raw power radiating from him.

The ropes bite into my wrists as I shift to look at him. My throat is dry, fear threatening to choke me, but I refuse to let it win. "We will find a way out of this," I tell him, forcing steel into my voice even as my hands shake. I need him to know I haven't given up – won't give up.

Sofia's laughter cuts through the warehouse like broken glass, bouncing off the walls and piercing my ears. "Hope is a luxury you cannot afford, darling." Her smile grows wider, more predatory. "The game is mine to win." She tosses the words at us like daggers, each one meant to draw blood.

Enzo's eyes find mine in the dim light. In that moment, something passes between us – something deeper than words. His gaze holds such fierce determination, such raw devotion, it makes my breath catch. Even bound and at Sofia's mercy, he radiates strength. I can read his silent vow in those hazel eyes: he won't let her take me from him.

The sounds outside grow louder – shouts and crashes that make the warehouse walls seem to vibrate. Sofia's head turns slightly toward the noise, but her confidence never wavers. Her heels click across the floor again as she moves toward the door, each step measured and deliberate.

The heavy metal door slams shut behind her with a finality that makes me flinch. Darkness presses in around us, broken only by the weak light filtering through the high windows. My heart pounds so hard I'm sure Enzo can hear it, each beat marking another second ticking away in this deadly game Sofia's playing.

giovanni's fury

...

dante falchetti

I lean against my office window, the weight of responsibility pressing down on my shoulders as I listen to Marco's raspy voice through the phone. The city lights blur beneath me, each flash a reminder of how quickly this situation has spiraled out of control.

"The Moretti warehouse?" My fingers tighten around the phone. "You're certain?"

"Positive, Mr. Falchetti. My guy spotted Sofia's men dragging your brother inside about an hour ago. They weren't exactly being subtle about it."

Fuck. My free hand curls into a fist. "What about the girl?"

"She's there too. Heard Sofia bragging about using her as bait." Marco pauses. "Look, they're not trying to hide. This feels like a trap."

"Everything with Sofia is a trap." I end the call, my jaw clenching as I process the information. The docks. Of course she'd choose somewhere isolated, somewhere she thinks she has the advantage.

My footsteps echo through the mansion's halls as I make my way to Father's study. The weight of this mess sits heavy in my gut. Enzo's always been reckless, but this – running headfirst into Sofia's territory for some waitress – it's beyond stupid.

I pause outside Father's study, memories of Lila flooding my mind unbidden. The way she challenged me from day one, refusing to be intimidated. How quickly she got under my skin and made me question everything. *Fuck*. Who am I to judge Enzo's stupidity when I fell just as hard?

My fingers brush over the ring box in my pocket – the one I've been carrying for weeks now. Lila's made it clear she's not ready, but I can't help wanting to make her mine completely. To wake up to her wild red hair spread across my pillow every morning, to build something real together.

"You're not thinking straight," she told me last night, curled against my chest. "The timing isn't right." Her fingers traced the scar along my jaw, eyes full of worry. "I love you, but I'm scared, Dante. Every time you leave, I wonder if you'll come back."

The weight of her words sits heavy in my chest. She's right – being with me puts a target on *her* back. Every rival family, every enemy I've made, they'd see her as leverage. Just like Sofia's using this waitress against Enzo now.

I think of Lila's studio in the east wing, how she's made it her sanctuary. The way paint always stains her hands, how she loses herself in her art for hours. She's carved out her own space in this violent world, but marriage would bind her to it permanently. No more pretending she could walk away if it got too dark.

"I want kids someday," I admitted to her last week, watching her sketch in bed. The thought of little ones with her fierce spirit and artist's soul... but Lila just shook her head.

"Our children would inherit your enemies," she whispered. "They'd never be truly safe."

The truth of it burns. I am what I am – the Family's enforcer, Giovanni Falchetti's ruthless right hand. Love doesn't change that. It just gives our enemies more ammunition.

My thoughts drift to the warehouse situation. Sofia Moretti won't hesitate to use anyone as leverage – she proved that by targeting Mia. And here I am, wanting to tie Lila even more closely to this dangerous life.

I press my palms against my eyes, trying to focus. Enzo needs me right now. I can't let my personal shit cloud my judgment. But standing here, thinking of Lila safely tucked away in her studio, I understand my brother's reckless charge into enemy territory. Love makes us stupid. Makes us vulnerable.

The ring box feels like it's burning a hole in my pocket. Maybe Lila's right to wait. Every time I put on my suit, strap on my gun, I know I might not come home. The thought of leaving her a widow, of our children growing up without a father... it's selfish to want that future when I can't guarantee I'll be there to protect them.

But fuck, I want it anyway. Want to see Lila in white, walking toward me. Want to watch her belly swell with our child. Want to build something real in this world of shadows and violence.

"You're brooding again," Lila would say if she saw me now, that knowing smirk on her face. She sees right through my walls, always has. Maybe that's why she knows better than to rush into marriage. She understands the weight of it better than I do.

I straighten my tie, squaring my shoulders. Time to focus on the crisis at hand. Sofia has my brother, and standing here dwelling on my own relationship drama won't help anyone.

I find Father behind his desk, the leather chair creaking as he turns to face me. One look at his expression and I know he's been stewing in his anger.

"Well?" His voice cuts through the silence.

"Marco confirmed it. They're at the Moretti warehouse by the docks. Both of them."

Father's fist slams against the mahogany desk. "This is on you, Dante! You were supposed to keep him in line!"

"With all due respect—" I stand my ground, meeting his glare. "Enzo's not some dog I can keep on a leash. He makes his own choices."

"Choices?" Father rises, his presence filling the room. "You let him get too close to that girl. You should have eliminated her the moment she became a liability!"

"And risk pushing Enzo further away?" My voice rises to match his. "He's already half out the door, treating every family decision like it's a personal attack. You know how he gets when he fixates on something."

"So you let him run straight into Sofia's hands?" Father's words drip with venom. "Your weakness for your brother has compromised this entire family!"

"My weakness?" I bark out a laugh. "You're the one who's been letting him get away with murder since he was a kid. Always the baby, always the special one who didn't have to follow the rules. And now you're surprised when he acts exactly like you taught him to?"

The silence that follows is deafening. Father's eyes narrow, decades of authority and control radiating from his stance.

"Watch yourself, Dante." His voice drops to a dangerous whisper. "Don't forget who you're talking to."

* * *

luca falchetti

I lean back in the leather chair of my father's study, memories flooding my mind as I process the news about Enzo. My law textbooks still gather dust on the shelves - a reminder of the life I almost chose. Three years of pre-law down the drain, but I don't regret it. Not when Dante showed me what real power looked like.

"You coming or what?" Dante's voice cuts through my thoughts. He stands in the doorway, that familiar dangerous glint in his eyes.

I nod, grabbing my gun from the desk drawer. "Wouldn't miss it. Enzo's family."

The word 'family' hits different when you're a Falchetti. I remember the day I decided to drop out of college - watching Dante command respect with just his presence. Books and legal briefs couldn't compete with that raw power. My professors talked about justice, but I saw real justice in how my cousins handled business.

"Remember that time in high school?" I ask as we head down the hallway. "When those punks tried to jump Enzo outside Mario's?"

Dante's lip quirks up slightly. "They never found all their teeth."

"The three of us were untouchable after that." Pride swells in my chest at the memory. "Everyone knew not to fuck with the Falchetti boys."

We step into Uncle Giovanni's office, where he's barking orders into his phone. The fear in the messenger's voice on the other end is obvious even from here. Good. We need that fear now more than ever.

"This shit with Sofia?" I crack my knuckles, anger building. "She needs to learn what happens when you touch our family."

Growing up, Enzo was more than just my cousin. He was the little brother I never had. While Dante taught me strength, Enzo showed me loyalty. The thought of him in Sofia's clutches makes my blood boil.

"The Morettis forgot who we are," I growl, checking my weapon. "They forgot what the Falchetti name means in this city."

Dante nods grimly. "Time to remind them."

I think back to our younger days - three cocky teenagers running these streets like we owned them. Because we did. The Falchetti name opened doors, commanded respect, struck fear. People stepped aside when we walked by.

"You know what Enzo told me when I quit school?" I look at Dante. "He said being a lawyer was noble, but being a Falchetti? That was power. Real power."

My hand instinctively touches the family crest tattoo on my chest. The same one all three of us got on my eighteenth birthday. Brotherhood sealed in ink and blood.

"We were legends back then," I say, memories of our wild teenage years flashing through my mind. "The whole city knew - you mess with one Falchetti, you get all of us."

Uncle Giovanni slams down his phone, finally acknowledging our presence. His eyes are cold, calculated. The look of a man ready for war.

"Sofia thinks she can break us by taking Enzo," I clench my fists. "She doesn't understand what family means to us."

The three of us - me, Dante, and Enzo - we weren't just cousins. We were brothers forged in the fire of this life. The same blood runs through our veins. The same loyalty burns in our hearts.

"They used to call us the three amigos," I say quietly, more to myself than anyone else. "But that wasn't quite right. We weren't friends. We were soldiers. Warriors."

I pull out my phone, scrolling through old photos. The three of us at family dinners, boxing matches, secret meetings. Always together. Always watching each other's backs.

"The fear we inspired then?" I look between Dante and Uncle Giovanni. "We need that now. Need to remind everyone why the Falchetti name carries weight."

The tension in Uncle Giovanni's study hits me like a physical force as I step into the doorway. My heart pounds against my ribs, but I keep my voice steady. "What can I do to help?"

Uncle Giovanni's eyes lock onto mine, then shift to Dante. The muscles in his jaw tighten. "You two need to come up with a plan fast. I've already dispatched a few of our top men to infiltrate the warehouse and eliminate the Moretti guards."

I watch as Giovanni continues barking orders into his phone, orchestrating the rescue operation. Taking advantage of his distraction, I lean closer to Dante, dropping my voice to barely above a whisper. "I've heard something about Sofia that could change things."

Dante's eyebrow arches with interest. "What is it?"

My pulse quickens as I share the intel I've gathered. "Sofia has a younger sister, Elara. She's been hitting up nightclubs, getting cozy with older men. Flying under the radar, but I've been watching. She could be Sofia's weak spot."

I see the wheels turning in Dante's mind as he processes this information. "And what do you plan to do with Elara?"

A smirk tugs at my lips as I lay out my strategy. "I'll seduce her, hold her for ransom. We can trade her for Enzo's safety. It could give us the upper hand against Sofia."

Dante's expression grows thoughtful, calculating. "Let's tread carefully, Luca. If we do this, we need to ensure it's foolproof. Elara's safety is paramount as well."

The gravity of what we're planning settles over us both. We huddle closer, speaking in hushed tones as we hash out the details. My mind races with possibilities – which clubs Elara frequents, how to orchestrate our "chance" meeting, the perfect way to draw her in without raising suspicion.

The study's atmosphere shifts from familial tension to calculated aggression. Standing beside Dante, I feel the weight of what we're about to do. This isn't just about saving Enzo anymore – it's about shifting the balance of power between our families.

Dante's eyes meet mine, and I see my own determination reflected there. No words are needed; we both understand what's at stake. The doubt that briefly crosses his features doesn't escape my notice, but like him, I push it aside. In our world, hesitation gets you killed.

breaking point
. . .

mia ricci

My heart pounds against my ribs as I track Sofia's every move. Her heels click across the concrete floor in a slow, deliberate rhythm that makes my skin crawl. Back and forth she paces, like a lioness sizing up her prey. The dim warehouse lights cast sinister shadows across her face, highlighting the cruel twist of her blood-red lips.

I can't help but notice she's attractive, in a sinister, almost vampiric way. Like some kind of *'Elvira'* imposter strutting through a B-grade horror film, with thick mascara and dramatic eye shadow that makes her gaze even more haunting. Her black hair falls in a sleek curtain down her back, and those eyes—they're so dark they seem to absorb light rather than reflect it. The contrast against her snow-white skin is jarring, almost theatrical, especially with those blood-red lips that curl into cruel smiles when she thinks she's got the upper hand.

Each step she takes sounds like a thunderclap in my ears. My breath catches when she pauses near Enzo, her manicured fingers trailing across the back of his chair. *What twisted scheme is she cooking up in that devious mind of hers?* The anticipation of her next move has my muscles coiled tight, ready to spring - though what good that would do with my hands bound, I don't know.

I do recall one night when Enzo and I were together, bathing in the tub at my apartment. Steam curled around us as we lounged in the warm water, his strong arms wrapped protectively around my waist. That's when he told me that Sofia Moretti once dated his brother, Dante. The revelation surprised me, though perhaps it shouldn't have - they both exuded that same dangerous magnetism. Enzo mentioned that Dante was 'hot' for her once upon a time, until her true personality came out - then she just became his 'crazy ex-girlfriend'. The way Enzo's jaw tightened when he spoke about her told me there was more to that story, but I didn't press. Some wounds, I was learning, were better left undisturbed.

Sofia's silence unnerves me more than her taunts. Her dark eyes narrow as she studies us, and I can practically see the gears turning behind that perfectly composed facade. Whatever she's planning, it won't be good. The malevolent gleam in her expression sends ice through my veins. She's going to hurt us - hurt him - and there's nothing I can do about it.

I steal another glance at Enzo beside me. Despite the blood trickling from the cut above his eye, he maintains that infuriating calm. His jaw is set, shoulders squared, meeting Sofia's gaze without flinching. But I see the crimson stain spreading across his white shirt, and my heart clenches. The urge to reach out, to press the hem of my shirt against his wounds, is overwhelming. But the zip ties bite into my wrists, keeping me frustratingly immobile.

The truth hits me like a physical blow as I watch him. ***I love him.*** The realization shouldn't shock me, but it does. After everything we've been through, after all his protection and sacrifices, I've fallen completely in love with Enzo Falchetti. The words burn on my tongue, desperate to be spoken. But I can't - not with Sofia hovering over us like a vulture, drinking in our every reaction. Not when saying it might give her another weapon to use against us.

My mind wanders back to the last time Enzo and I had sex. I was on top of him, rocking my hips back and forth, lost in the rhythm of our bodies moving as one. His hands were on my breasts, his touch igniting a fire within me that spread through every nerve. The sensation of his thick cock inside me was overwhelming, filling me completely and driving me to the edge of ecstasy. I thought I had died and gone to heaven when I experienced the best climax of my life. It was more than just sex between us that night; it was a joining of our hearts, a deep connection and bond that would never be broken. His gaze locked onto mine, and at that moment, I knew that we were more than just lovers—we were each other's sanctuary—and ended our night with long, open-mouthed kisses to solidify our union.

An explosion rocks the warehouse, making me jump in my restraints. The chaos outside has escalated into what sounds like an all-out war. Gunfire echoes through the metal walls, accompanied by shouts and the occasional earth-shaking blast. The concrete floor vibrates beneath my feet with each detonation. Another burst of automatic weapons fire, closer this time, followed by the distinct sound of breaking glass. The battle rages on without pause, and I wonder if we're about to be caught in the crossfire.

Sofia's composure cracks slightly at a particularly loud explosion. Her perfect eyebrows draw together as she glances toward the warehouse entrance. For a split second, uncertainty flashes across her features before she masks it with renewed determination. She stalks closer to us, her movements more predatory than ever.

"Your family thinks they can save you," she spits at Enzo, venom dripping from every word. "But they're too late."

I watch fresh blood trickle down Enzo's temple, my fingers itching to reach for him. He doesn't respond to Sofia's taunt, but I notice the slight tension in his shoulders, the way his hands flex against his restraints. Whatever's happening outside has him on edge, despite his outward calm.

I love him.

I've been utterly captivated by him from the start. The electricity between us is palpable. Just one smirk from him and my body responds, growing slick with desire. I shut my eyes, recalling the first moment I saw him in that diner. Our gazes locked, and I found myself unable to look away. The urge to press my lips against his was overwhelming—and I hadn't even learned his name! It was pointless to deny it; whenever he was near, all I could think about was perching on his lap, tracing kisses along his neck while he explored my body—a favorite form of foreplay that he seemed to instinctively understand. I adored watching him undo my bra, slowly pulling the fabric down with his teeth, as if we were sharing an intimate peep show meant only for each other. And his mouth … *oh,* his expertise in licking me … teasing my nipples to death until they're rock-hard and erect in his mouth. I would wither underneath his grip, straining to unzip his pants, but he wouldn't let me—not until he'd hear me moan and beg by his ear.

The gunfire intensifies, and now I can hear the distinct sound of fighting - flesh hitting flesh, grunts of pain, the thud of bodies hitting the ground. Sofia's men shout orders and obscenities, their voices tight with panic. Another explosion rocks the building, closer than ever, and dust rains down from the ceiling. The light fixtures swing wildly, casting crazy shadows that dance across the walls.

"Boss!" One of Sofia's men bursts through the door, his face pale. "They're—"

A bullet catches him in the shoulder before he can finish, spraying blood across the metal door. He crumples with a cry of pain as Sofia whirls toward the entrance, pulling a sleek pistol from her jacket. Her perfectly controlled facade has finally cracked, replaced by raw fury as she backs toward us.

The sounds of chaos outside grow louder with each passing second. Gunshots crack through the air like thunder, followed by screams that make my blood run cold. My heart pounds against my ribs as I watch Sofia's face contort with rage when one of her men bursts in.

"They've killed Paulie and Vincent!" he shouts before disappearing back into the fray.

"Those fucking Falchetti bastards," Sofia snarls, her perfectly manicured hand tightening around her pistol. The composed mask she's worn all night finally cracks, revealing the monster beneath.

She stalks toward Enzo like a predator, each click of her heels against the concrete floor making me flinch. Without warning, she whips her gun across his face. The sickening crack of metal meeting flesh echoes through the room, and I bite back a scream.

Blood trickles down Enzo's cheek, but his eyes remain defiant. He spits at her feet, a mixture of blood and saliva staining her expensive shoes. "That all you've got?"

"You arrogant piece of shit." Sofia's control snaps completely. She strikes him again and again, the pistol becoming a brutal instrument in her hands. Each impact draws fresh blood, but Enzo refuses to cry out.

"Fucking die already!" she screams, her perfectly styled hair coming loose as she rains down blow after blow.

I can't take it anymore. The ropes dig into my wrists as I thrash against them. "STOP! PLEASE STOP!" My voice breaks, tears streaming down my face. I can't watch him die. Not like this. Not because of me.

Sofia pauses, turning to face me. Her smile is pure evil, blood spattering her designer blouse. "No."

She returns to Enzo with renewed fury, striking him until his head lolls forward. Blood drips steadily onto the floor, forming a dark pool at his feet. My heart shatters seeing him so still, so broken.

The warehouse falls silent except for my ragged breathing and Sofia's heels as she turns toward me. Her chest heaves from the exertion, mascara smeared beneath wild eyes. Slowly, deliberately, she raises the gun until the cold metal presses against my temple.

Her finger tightens on the trigger. "Say goodbye, little waitress."

the hunt begins
. . .

luca falchetti

The bass from *Club Euphoria* still pulses through my veins as I step into the crisp night air. Amber - or was it Ashley? - slips her number into my pocket, her perfume lingering as she whispers promises of a wild night. Any other time, I'd be all over that invitation. But tonight isn't about pleasure.

I check my phone. Three clubs down, no sign of Elara Moretti. The photo I have of her doesn't do her justice according to my sources - they say she's a knockout with those signature Moretti blue eyes. My intel better be solid about her Friday night habits, or this whole operation goes sideways.

"You sure you don't want company?" Amber/Ashley calls from the club entrance, her voice carrying that perfect mix of suggestion and need that usually hits all my buttons.

I flash her my practiced smile, the one that makes women weak in the knees. "Rain check, beautiful. Business calls."

The disappointment on her face almost makes me reconsider. Almost. But Enzo's life hangs in the balance, and Sofia Moretti needs to learn she can't fuck with our family.

My Audi purrs to life as I pull up the next location on my phone - *Club Venom*. The bouncer there owes me a favor, which might come in handy if Elara shows up. I navigate through downtown's maze of one-way streets, my mind racing through scenarios of how to approach her when I find her.

Too aggressive, she'll bolt. Too subtle, she might not take the bait. I need to play this perfectly - be the charming stranger who catches her eye but doesn't seem to know or care about her family connections. The kind of guy who makes her want to break her own rules.

The line outside *Venom* stretches around the block, but I park right up front. The privileged perks of being a Falchetti in this city. Women in the queue eye my car, then me as I step out. Their interest is obvious, but I barely notice. My focus narrows to the mission at hand.

Mike, the bouncer, gives me a slight nod as I approach. "Mr. Falchetti."

"Busy night?" I ask, slipping him an envelope thick with cash. "Need intel on someone who might show up."

His massive frame shifts closer, voice dropping. "Already here. VIP section, far corner. Wearing red."

My pulse quickens. Finally. I smooth down my jacket and head inside, the thrumming music washing over me. The crowd parts as I move through - there's something about the way I carry myself that makes people instinctively clear a path. Years of training, of knowing I'm untouchable in these spaces.

The VIP section rises above the main floor, offering a perfect view of the writhing masses below. I scan the elevated booths until I spot a flash of red. My breath catches.

The intelligence photos didn't do Elara justice at all. She's perched on the edge of her seat, laughing at something her friend is saying. That red bustier hugs every curve, her dark hair falling in waves past her shoulders. But it's her eyes that grab me - electric blue, just like they said, but with something soft and vulnerable in them that the photos couldn't capture.

For a moment, I forget why I'm here. Forget about Enzo, about Sofia, about the whole damn vendetta. I just want to know what makes this girl laugh, what thoughts swirl behind those striking eyes.

But then reality crashes back. She's a *Moretti*. A means to an end. Nothing more.

I make my way to the bar, positioning myself in her line of sight. Order a whiskey neat, though I won't drink it. Need my head clear tonight. I can feel her gaze land on me - women always look, and I've learned to sense it. But I don't acknowledge her yet. Let her wonder, let her interest build.

The bartender slides my drink over. I raise it slightly, taking in the amber liquid, aware of Elara's continued attention. Every move I make is calculated now, a careful dance of seduction and strategy. I've done this countless times before, but never with stakes this high.

The music shifts to something slower, more sensual. Perfect timing. I turn slightly, letting my eyes meet hers across the space between us. Hold the contact for three seconds - long enough to show interest, short enough to leave her wanting more. Then I look away, take a sip of my whiskey.

Elara moves through the crowd with an ethereal grace, her dark hair catching the strobe lights. But there's something else, something that makes my gut twist. She's clearly high, pupils dilated as she sways to the music.

I hang back in the shadows, watching her dance. She's uninhibited, sensual, moving between partners like she's searching for something she can't find. Male, female - it doesn't seem to matter. But beneath the drug-induced euphoria, I catch glimpses of desperation in her movements. The high is wearing off.

Mimo, my usual dealer contact, lurks near the bar. I make my way over, keeping Elara in my peripheral vision. "That's my sale tonight," I tell him, sliding several hundred across the counter. His eyes widen at the stack of bills, but he knows better than to argue with a Falchetti.

I position myself in a dimly lit corner, waiting. It doesn't take long. Elara approaches, her movements becoming more erratic as withdrawal sets in. Up close, she's even more striking - all delicate features and those striking blue eyes that pierce through me despite their drug-hazed state.

"Mimo said you could help me out," she says, her voice husky and uncertain.

My mouth goes dry. The physical pull between us is immediate and intense, catching me completely off guard. Heat floods my veins as she steps closer, her floral perfume mixing with the scent of sweat and vodka. This wasn't part of the plan. I'm supposed to be cold, calculating - not fighting the urge to run my fingers through her hair and taste those full lips.

"I've got what you need," I manage to say, but the words feel thick in my throat. Duty wars with desire as I watch her nibble her lower lip nervously. Christ, this job just got a lot more complicated.

I let my gaze drift over her, taking in every detail. The red bustier she wears accentuates her curves perfectly, and I have to force myself to stay focused. Her presence is magnetic, drawing me in despite my best efforts to maintain professional distance. My breath catches as she shifts closer, the strobe lights casting shadows across her delicate features.

"You're new," she says, tilting her head. Her voice carries a hint of suspicion beneath the need. "I haven't seen you here before."

I keep my expression neutral, though my pulse races. "I move around. Different clubs, different crowds." The lie falls easily from my lips, practiced and smooth. "But tonight, I'm right where I need to be."

She studies me with those striking blue eyes, and for a moment, I see a flash of clarity cutting through the drug-induced haze. There's intelligence there, sharp and assessing despite her current state. It catches me off guard - another complication I hadn't anticipated.

"I'm where I need to be, too," she says slurring her words and chuckling to herself. Her delicate fingers wrap around the glass in front of her, and I notice the slight tremor in her hand. The drugs are hitting her system hard - exactly what I need for this to work, even if something in my chest tightens at the sight of Elara Moretti so vulnerable.

I lean against the wall, letting the shadows play across my features. "First time I've seen you here," I say, keeping my voice low and inviting.

"I get around," Elara replies with a coy smile. She sways closer, and I catch another whiff of her expensive perfume beneath the club's heavy atmosphere. "Though I haven't seen you before either. I'd remember someone like you."

My heart hammers against my ribs. Even in her altered state, there's something magnetic about her - an innocent vulnerability that wars with a wild spark in those blue eyes. I force myself to remember why I'm here, what's at stake. Enzo's life depends on this working.

"Maybe we were meant to meet tonight," I say, letting my gaze drift over her face. Her pupils are wide, dark pools that can't quite focus. The responsible part of me wants to get her help, not exploit this situation. But I can't afford morals right now.

She leans in closer, her fingers brushing my arm. "Maybe we were." Her words slur slightly. "But unfortunately, I should probably go. I'm... out of funds for the evening."

This is my opening. I try to ignore how my stomach twists as I reach into my pocket, making sure she sees the small packet. "That doesn't have to be a problem. My car's right outside. We could continue this conversation somewhere more—*private*. Head for the coke?"

Elara's eyes lock onto the packet, and I see the internal struggle play across her features. Desire wars with hesitation. She bites her lower lip, and I find myself tracking the movement before I can stop myself.

"A blow job? I don't usually..." she starts, but her eyes never leave my hand.

"One second of bravery," I murmur, letting my free hand brush her waist. "That's all it takes. Let me take care of you tonight."

The Hunt Begins

The rational part of my brain screams that this is wrong on so many levels. But when she looks up at me through those long lashes, I'm caught in a web of my own making. The mission blurs with genuine attraction, and I'm no longer sure where one ends and the other begins.

"Okay," she whispers, and steps closer. "Your car?"

I take her hand, ignoring how perfectly it fits in mine, how her touch sends electricity through my veins. As I lead her toward the exit, my mind races with the implications of what I'm about to do. The weight of the zip ties in my pocket feels heavier with each step.

Just before we reach the door, she squeezes my hand and pulls me to a stop. My heart freezes - has she sensed something's wrong? But when I turn, her eyes are soft with something that looks dangerously close to trust.

"I just wanted to say..." she starts, swaying slightly. "You seem different. Not like the others."

The words hit me like a physical blow. Because in this moment, as I lead her into a trap, I'm exactly like all the others who've taken advantage of her vulnerability. Maybe worse.

But I can't back out now. Enzo's life hangs in the balance. So I squeeze her hand back and give her my most reassuring smile, even as guilt churns in my gut.

"Let's go," I say softly, pushing open the club's door. The cool night air hits us like a wake-up call, and Elara shivers. Without thinking, I shrug off my jacket and drape it over her shoulders.

She looks up at me with those impossibly blue eyes, and for a moment, I forget to breathe. "Such a gentleman," she murmurs.

My car waits in the shadows of the parking lot, and with each step closer, my resolve weakens. The zip ties in my pocket feel like they're burning a hole through the fabric. Looking at her trusting face, I realize I've never hated myself more.

But before I can reconsider, she stumbles slightly on her heels. I catch her instinctively, and she falls against my chest with a soft laugh. Her warmth seeps through my shirt, and suddenly the night feels electric with possibility—and danger.

Continued...

you might also like

the dark side of him

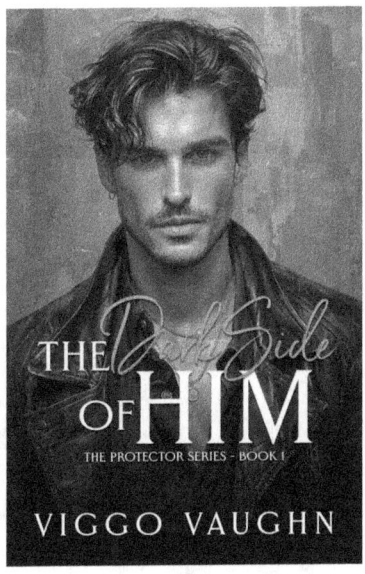

love ignites. loyalty crumbles. danger explodes.

Lila Rossi, an artist with a thirst for life, gets tangled in a deadly underworld war after witnessing a brutal mob hit. Now, she's a target, and the ruthless enforcer **Dante Falchetti** is her only protection.

Dante is a man of shadows with a past as dark as his suits. He's bound by duty, yet Lila's fiery spirit sparks an unexpected flame.

Lila: Trapped in a world of violence, she finds solace in the forbidden allure of her protector. But can love bloom amidst the threat of mob executions?

As danger escalates, the line between protector and desired blurs.

Can they survive the storm brewing around them, or will their secrets and desires consume them both?

Delve into a world of

- Gritty Mob Warfare
- Steamy Forbidden Romance
- Heart-stopping Suspense

The Protector Series - Book 1

Ebook & Paperback

read next

Tangled Loyalties

🔥 blood calls to blood... 🔥

Sofia Moretti, the ruthless head of the Moretti crime family, has captured Enzo Falchetti. But this isn't just a game of power. It's a war.

When Elara Moretti, Sofia's sister, is kidnapped by the rival Falchetti family, the stakes skyrocket. Delivered into the hands of Luca Falchetti, a man whose cousin's fate now hangs in the balance, Elara becomes a pawn in a deadly game of revenge.

Trapped with her enemy, Elara finds herself drawn to Luca, a man of shadows and steel. Their forbidden attraction ignites a dangerous passion, blurring the lines between love and hate.

But in the Mafia, love is the deadliest weapon of all.

Can Elara trust the man who holds her freedom in his hands? Will Luca choose family loyalty or the woman who's become his exquisite torment?

The Protector Series - Book 3

Available in

Ebook & Paperback

the bargain bride

By V. Vaughn

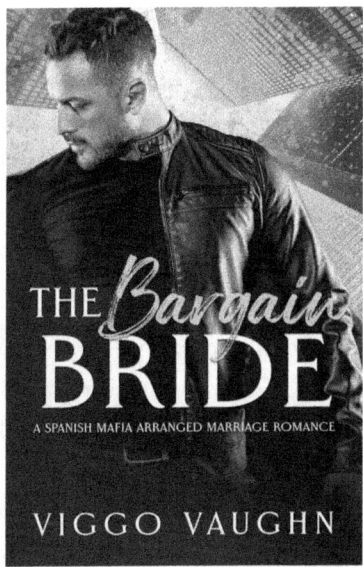

grease, grit, and a dangerous proposition

Chelsea Jenkins is a woman who knows how to fix a flat tire and a failing business. But when a notorious **Mafia heir** sets up shop across the street, sparks fly hotter than a welding torch.

Victor Morales is all about fast cars, loose women, and keeping his father's criminal empire humming. The last thing he needs is a fiery mechanic throwing wrenches in his plans.

But desperation has a way of changing the game. When Chelsea stumbles upon a shocking secret, Victor makes her an offer she can't refuse.

Love? Never part of the deal.

Survival? A high-octane gamble.

The Bargain Bride is a story where danger simmers beneath the grease, and love takes a reckless turn for the unexpected.

Get ready for a wild ride!

A Spanish Mafia Arranged Marriage Romance
Ebook & Paperback

second in command

1977 new york

Francesca Donato was twenty-one, and in her prime. Gorgeous, wild, an Italian princess. Her father, second in command under Vincenzio Benedetti the *Capo* of the Montagna Mafia family, spoiled his daughter to extremes where she always got what she wanted. Designer clothes, exotic cars and money, Francesca wanted Enzo, a soldier in the Benedetti army.

Enzo Andonetto was untamed, out of control and trigger happy. Nightclubs, dancing and drugs were always on the menu when he spotted Francesca dancing one night at the club with her friends.

Apart, they were lively, but together, they were a force, and Vincenzio welcomed their union when Enzo asked his permission to marry her.

But there was one test the Capo needed Enzo to do before his wedding, get rid of a rival that was stealing from their territory.

How does an unmatched pair climax? By violence, and an unexpected gunshot that came from nowhere…

An Italian Mafia Arranged Marriage Romance

Includes crossover characters from "*Evenly Matched*"

Ebook & Paperback

evenly matched

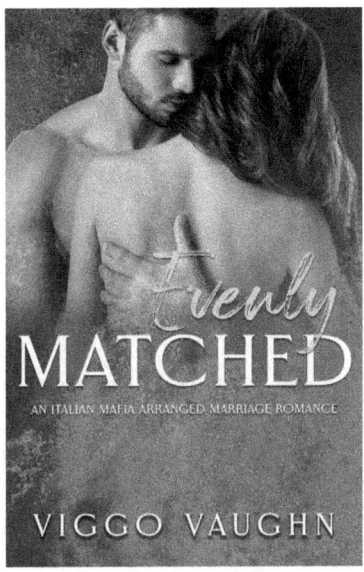

Lorenzo Beneditti was his mother's favorite but his father's constant source of trouble. The Beneditti family was well known throughout many organized crime families; they were considered top-level, the peak of the Italian Mob. At twenty-two, Lorenzo repeatedly tried to live up to his father's expectations but always fell short—until he met his match in the female version of himself.

Carla Caldarelli was her father's favorite but her mother's worst nightmare. The Caldarelli family were soldiers of the Beneditti's—second in command—so when Carla finds herself in a bind, she looks to Lorenzo for help.

Can Lorenzo save Carla? Can Carla rescue Lorenzo?

Includes crossover characters from *"The Bargain Bride"*

An Italian Mafia Arranged Marriage Romance

Ebook & Paperback

about viggo vaughn

Viggo Vaughn is an emerging author of Mafia Romance, Mystery/Suspense and Thrillers. Viggo has many writing interests and lives an incognito digital lifestyle.

Viggo is part of the Ardent Artist Books family and is currently the author of several books.

youtube.com/theardentartist
amazon.com/stores/Ardent-Artist-Books/author/B08BX8F1DZ

also by viggo vaughn

CROSSOVER•CHARACTERS

The Bargain Bride - Book 1

Evenly Matched - Book 2

Second in Command - Book 3

THE•PROTECTOR•SERIES

The Dark Side of Him - Book 1

Guarded by Shadows - Book 2

Tangled Loyalties - Book 3

www.ingramcontent.com/pod-product-compliance
Lightning Source LLC
LaVergne TN
LVHW012023060526
838201LV00061B/4427